Renee 3:

Long Live the Queen

Renee 3:

Long Live the Queen

Brandie Davis

www.urbanbooks.net

Urban Books, LLC
300 Farmingdale Road, NY-Route 109
Farmingdale, NY 11735

Renee 3: Long Live the Queen

ISBN 13: 978-1-64556-109-5
ISBN 10: 1-64556-109-7

First Trade Paperback Printing August 2020
Printed in the United States of America

10 9 8 7 6 5 4 3 2 1

This is a work of fiction. Any references or similarities to actual events, real people, living or dead, or to real locales are intended to give the novel a sense of reality. Any similarity in other names, characters, places, and incidents is entirely coincidental.

Distributed by Kensington Publishing Corp.
Submit Orders to:
Customer Service
400 Hahn Road
Westminster, MD 21157-4627
Phone: 1-800-733-3000
Fax: 1-800-659-2436

I dedicate this book to my mother.

I love you.

Prologue

Watching Dane, the hard assassin who mentored and introduced Renee to the drug world, with her family made Renee want one of her own. Such things as visiting relatives' homes, where you gossiped, laughed, ate dinners, and connected, made Renee wish she had kept her uncle Lyfe around and not killed him in that fire. While sleeping in Dane's aunt Laura's guest room, Renee would stay up all hours of the night imagining how life would have been had her mother loved her, her father never died, and her sister Page been halfway sane. She thought long and hard about the what-ifs and listened to the nights Dane escaped from her family's home and did her killings. She listened to the cries she and her aunt poured out the night they killed Dane's brother-in-law, Benz. That was the night that shook Renee to the core simply because it had proven that every woman she knew was cursed just like her.

Back home in the comfort of her own bed, Renee listened to the sound of Julian's heartbeat. There was nothing more soothing than resting her head on her childhood love's chest and listening to his very existence. Thoughts of marriage and motherhood walked their way into her mind and took a seat. It surprised her how at ease she became once she painted a picture of her very own family. She was surprised twice as much when she heard herself expressing these emotions to Julian.

"What if we gave it a try?"

"Gave what a try?"

"Getting married and having kids."

Julian sat Renee up so that he could look at her. "Where is this coming from?"

"From here." She pointed to her heart, the strongest muscle in her body that leaked out love.

Gazing into Renee's eyes, he saw the woman he fell in love with who'd fought to come out of her dark corner. He saw his lover and friend, the reason for his existence. When she smiled at him, he saw the woman he betrayed.

"So what do you think?" she asked, pulling him out of his guilt-ridden thoughts.

"I think it's gonna happen, as long as you forgive me."

"Forgive you for what?"

Julian failed the first time he tried to come clean and expose that he had slept with Carmen before either of them had known she was Renee's half-sister, the love child Renee's father created out of adultery, so now Julian refused to fail at coming clean again.

"Renee, when I went to Jamaica to speak with Dane, I—"

"Renee! Get down here!"

The urgency in Dane's voice caused Renee and Julian to look at each other in confusion and exit the room. As frustrating as it was to be interrupted for the second time he tried to tell his secret, Julian was relieved that Dane announced herself. The last thing he wanted was to spill his guts when they weren't alone. The conversation was personal, between him and Renee, and no other person's input or opinion was welcomed.

The couple walked down the stairs, and their vision took in Dane standing directly in front of Tina, the gossip queen herself. Julian felt his mind blacking in and out. The last he had seen of Tina was in photos taken by people he'd had follow her. After putting a hit out on a man who used to work for him, Waves, he dropped the ball and never got around to shutting Tina's trap for good.

"What are you doing here?" Julian growled. In protective mode, he stood in front of Renee.

Renee's eyes never left Tina as she tried to figure out who she was.

"I'd like to know the same thing. I found her standing in front of the door on my way here," Dane chimed in, Renee's house keys clutched in her hand.

The color was drained from Tina's face, and her heart was racing. The look in Dane's eyes made Tina uneasy, and she slightly regretted coming to Renee's home. All eyes were on her. Her brain told her to speak, but her mouth wouldn't comply.

"I suggest you answer him," Dane warned.

Terrified, Tina opened her mouth, and words finally fell out. They tripped over one another, and Tina stuttered with every word she formed. Midsentence, she stopped, closed her eyes, and took a deep breath while telling herself, *relax and tell them what you know.*

"There's something I think you should know." Tina looked around Julian, her sight landing on Renee.

Julian never moved from in front of Renee, his stance giving off the impression that if he did, she would be in danger. She stepped from behind him, her touch letting him know that it was okay.

"I don't recollect ever meeting you, so what could you possibly have to tell me?" Renee asked.

"I know you don't know me, but I think you should know that your sister, Carmen, can't be trusted."

Tina was holding her breath while waiting for a response from Renee. However, the only thing Renee did was play a game of "don't blink." She gave off no indication of whether she was angry.

Seconds passed before she finally replied, "What do you know?"

Dane walked over to the door and guarded it as reassurance that Tina would tell them everything she knew before leaving.

"I know that the second you retire, she is going to take a hit out on you. From the moment she met you, her plans were to suck you dry, then dispose of you. Carmen envies you. She'll do anything to take your place and be queen of New York's drug world."

"You're the one who told Page about me." Things were piecing themselves together in Renee's mind. The lingering question of how her psycho sister knew where to find her in order to try to murder her was now answered.

Surprised by her comment, all of the strength Tina had mustered up to speak rapidly deteriorated. "Yes, I am. And I'm sorry about that. I had no idea what her intentions were."

"So you understand why I am wary of you. How do I know you didn't tell anyone else?"

"I promise I didn't!" Tina walked closer to Renee. She needed her to believe that she told no one else about her identity. "I know I don't have the best reputation, but I'm trying to right my wrongs. Instead of my mouth hurting people, I'm trying to actually help for a change," she lied.

There was nothing positive about what Tina wanted to do. She had two goals in mind and two goals only. The first was to expose Carmen as payback for giving her up to Jared, and the second was to get both of them off her back. To see the damage Jared did to her body whenever she looked in the mirror was heartbreaking. Before those two came into her life, things were decent, and now all she wanted was for things to go back to the way they were. If she wanted any type of normalcy, she had to fight fire with fire and get Carmen and Jared out of her life for good.

Renee didn't respond. The silence only heard in libraries filled the room and caused Tina's teeth to chatter. She had no idea what ran through Renee's head, and the suspense was killing her until Dane opened her mouth and spoke up.

"I want proof. I trust no one who runs in the same circles as Carmen."

Tina jammed her hand into her back pocket and pulled out her phone. She pushed the touch screen, and the device played the conversation between her and Carmen.

"I never knew Jordan had another sister." Everyone in the room listened to Tina set off the conversation, all while referring to Renee under her alias.

"Neither did I. We didn't find out about each other until my uncle told us a few months back. In Miami, I was a kept woman while she was running all of New York. Ain't that about a bitch?"

"What's wrong with that?"

"Everything. Like a princess, I had everything given to me and thought I had my shit together, but I was given a reality check when I seen how she was living. Have you ever seen her home? It's gorgeous. Fit for a queen. If it weren't for my uncle laying it all out for me, I would have never believed she acquired all of those things alone. The only time I even achieved half of that wealth was through my ex. I got nothing on my own, so seeing how she lived made me want to be a boss. Her success made me want to stop being a princess and start being a queen, but I refuse to start from the bottom, so I set out to gain her trust and take what I deserve. But things didn't turn out that way. Before I had a chance to fully slither into her life, she crowned me her protégé after I saved her from being killed by the hands of her sister."

"That's a good thing. Now you don't have to go through all that trouble."

"Yeah, it's a good thing, but still work must be done. Because even though she's handing everything to me, I still have to get rid of her once she retires. I can't risk her taking it all back and coming back for—"

"Cut it off," Renee instructed.

Although Renee had made up her mind and considered Carmen dead seconds into the recording, she still had an apology to give Julian and Dane. From the very beginning, they had seen Carmen for who she was and had warned her, but still, she chose to ignore them and believe what she wanted. Now that everything was out in the open, she had to apologize.

"I'm sorry," she said. Her eyes were stationed on the front door.

"Who are you apologizing to?" Julian asked.

"To you and Dane. You both tried to warn me, so what better time to apologize?"

No one spoke, but the silence alerted Renee that her soulmate and best friend accepted her apology.

"How did you meet Carmen? She's fairly new to New York. Was that your first interaction with her?" Dane asked.

Things were running smoothly, but Tina's nerves were still in disarray. Her legs were shaking, and she feared she'd collapse at any minute. "May I?" she asked, pointing to the couch.

Renee nodded her head, and Tina's spaghetti legs wobbled their way across the room. She took a seat. Her hands were full of sweat, so she placed her phone down and thoroughly wiped her hands on her jeans.

"That wasn't the first time we met. The first time we met, we were at a club, and she wanted to know if I knew any men who were willing to put in work. I let her know that all the guys I knew about were killed a few months back. However, there was one I told her about."

Tina's head dropped, and her hands began to shake. Everyone noticed how uneasy she was and waited for her to finish. When moments passed without another word leaving her mouth, Renee stepped in. Her tone was soothing and caring.

"Who did you tell her about, Tina?"

She sat down beside her and rubbed her back in order to calm her down. Because of her kind gesture, Tina felt a little more willing to tell her about Jared and not fear so much for her life.

"I told her about Jared."

They all tried to fight it, but their laughter slipped through their lips.

"Obviously, you're not up on your current events like we all thought. Renee's psychotic lovesick puppy is dead," Dane chuckled.

"No, I'm ahead of it," Tina whispered. "He's not dead. I know a nurse in the hospital he was treated at who can verify that."

The way Tina spoke caused the laughter to die down and everyone to look at each other. Tina removed her shades, her face a long way from being back to normal.

"He found out I told Carmen he was alive, and he did this to me." She pointed to her bruises. "Today, Carmen asked me if I knew anything about you and Jared killing her crew, and I recorded it. I have a feeling she thinks you're on to her."

Dane rushed toward Tina, her knee-high boots stomping against the floor. "This shit coming out of your mouth will get you killed. My men got rid of Jared's body, and there's no way he's alive."

Once again, Tina's heart rate sped up, but she needed Jared taken care of just like she needed Carmen gone, so she pushed herself to tell everything that needed to be told. "It's true. He's walking and breathing just like everyone in this room."

Dane was a true believer that if someone lied, they did not look you in the eye. Never once during this debate did Tina turn away. She tried to fight what her conscience was telling her, but she knew there was no running away from this one. Fergus and Calloway, her most trusted work twins, had lied to her.

"What do you want?" Renee intervened.

Julian stood against the wall, his eyes staring a hole into the ceiling. *The more things change, the more they stay the same,* sprinted through his mind.

"I don't understand," Tina said.

"Nothing is for free, especially this information. So what do you want?"

It's now or never, Tina thought. "I want them out of my life. I want you to do what you do best. After what Jared's done to me, I'm living in fear, and it's all because of Carmen, so I need them to go away."

For the first time since she'd been there, Tina looked at peace as she told Renee her wish. Even though all of her information was accurate, Renee didn't believe for a minute she was telling her all of this out of the goodness of her heart, but she was just happy that Tina finally admitted it.

"Consider it done."

Tina observed Renee. She needed to see for herself whether she was serious. When she never blinked an eye, she knew Renee was the real deal.

"Thank you!"

Tina jumped into Renee's arms, showing her her appreciation for giving her her life back, squeezing her like a child squeezes a teddy bear. Renee stared at Julian until he looked down from the ceiling. The cold, withdrawn look told him everything he needed to know. Instead of looking at Dane, he walked past her, his shoulder grazing hers, an indication that they had business to take care of.

He opened the door, and Dane walked through it. She stood in the hall, waiting for Tina to exit.

Renee backed out of Tina's hold and continued to speak. "Thank you for coming here to warn me about Carmen. That took a lot of guts. But you no longer have to worry. They'll be taken care of," Renee reassured her.

Tina smiled, a weight lifted off her shoulders. "Thank you."

Renee returned her smile and walked Tina to the door. "They will take you home. Take care, Tina."

Tina smiled at Renee once more before leaving her sight. Dane followed close behind her when she left the house.

Julian leaned into Renee, their arms wrapping around each other in a tight embrace.

"Kill them all, Tina and the twins included. And make sure to make it as painful as possible," she whispered in his ear.

"I will. I'm going to do what I should have done a long time ago. Should have killed them without hesitation the moment I smelled a rat."

The two kissed with the thought of starting a family lingering in both their minds. Renee watched Julian walk farther into the hall, and when he was out of sight, she went back into her home. She walked through the living room, and her eye caught a glimpse of Tina's phone resting on the couch. Picking it up, she flicked through it until she found the conversation between Tina and Carmen. She listened to the conversation Tina had played for her and became angry with herself for not discovering Carmen's true colors sooner. Each word made her laugh at how naive she had been, but when the recording kept going when it should have ended, her eyebrows caved in, and her heart fell to her feet as she listened to the remainder of the recording.

"I can't risk her taking it all back, can't risk her coming back for Julian."

"Julian?"

"Her best friend, her partner, her lover. Before I found out that she goes by this alias Jordan, I met Julian while vacationing in Jamaica. Instantly, we were attracted to one another and had wild sex. I never thought I'd see him again, but life has a funny way of making things happen, because there he was, sharing a bed with my sister. An additional thing I added on my must-have list."

"It's suicide what you're trying to do, Carmen, pure suicide."

"Only if I get caught."

The phone slipped from Renee's hand and exploded against the floor. She watched the shattered screen and broken case scatter before she diverted her attention to the front door. Her cotton socks sank into the carpet as the muscles in her legs tightened and pushed out with every forceful sprint.

What the fuck did Tina not tell me?

She hurled open the wooden door, and the door-knob smashed against the wall and stuck. Renee's wide eyes hungrily searched down the long, well-decorated, pristine, museum mimic of a hallway and saw nothing. Dashing back inside her penthouse of horror, her feet leaped onto the stairs she now regretted existed.

You can still catch them.

Her bedroom never seemed so far, and her body never pushed so hard, yet it felt like light years passed with every second. Inside the dark room, she threw herself on the terrace, her chest pushed into her hands as she gripped the railing. The tip of her toes granted her height.

It was the most vacant view New York had ever supplied. No souls inhabited the streets or drove cars polluting the air. No dogs were being walked. There were no signs of life being lived. It was only darkness, a clip taken from the film *I Am Legend*. Determined to hear the words Tina never spoke, Renee grabbed her cell phone from her pocket and impatiently waited for Julian's voice to replace the ringing.

"Please leave your message for—"

Renee quickly hung up and punched Julian's name again.

"Please leave your message for—"

She repeatedly dialed Julian's number. Hearing no voice other than the female recording's, she changed route and tried Dane.

"Leave a message."

Their phones are off, so they want no interruptions.

"Leave a message." Again, she tried and tried and, in the process, lost count of how many times her calls were denied.

"Leave a message." She spoke to Renee in slow motion, clear, and with a hint of amusement in the mechanical voice. The words duplicated themselves in Renee's mind until there was no more room for them to live. *Leave a message, leave a message, leave a message . . .*

Renee's fingers covered the phone, and with the strength of her right arm and the emotions of her heart, she threw it into the glass door. From the center of the door, a crack grew into a spider. Long legs stretched to each end of the door, and then it exploded. Big and small pieces of glass attacked Renee. After cutting into her arms and face, it covered the floor. Attempting to aide her cheeks, Renee's fingers fell into open wounds. She hid behind her hands, and tears tumbled out of her eyes and burned the gashes.

"It's not true," she mumbled.

The terrace grew small, and the cold, teeth-chattering air turned dry.

"I think it's gonna happen, as long as you forgive me."

"Forgive you for what?"

"Renee, when I went to Jamaica to speak with Dane, I—"

Renee sat stiff, her eyes large and the past flashing before her.

It all makes sense, Julian wanting Carmen out of our lives and Carmen's obsession with wanting what didn't belong to her. "Fuck," Renee mumbled. She fidgeted and looked around. Renee's mind swarmed with thoughts while she constantly repeated, "Fuck, fuck, fuck, fuck." The curses grew louder, one after the other. Her inability to calm down and release her anger forced her to her feet.

"Fuck! Fuck! Fuuuuuccccckkkkkk!" she yelled. Her body erect and hands balled into fists, Renee screamed into the night sky. The small number of people now roaming the streets looked up at the building disrupting the peace. Renee didn't stop screaming until the air in her lungs dissolved and a faint, small sound impersonating a scream came out. She banged her back against the railing and slid down the metal, where she sat on the ground, tears flowing down her cheeks. Heavy sobs formed in the pit of Renee's stomach and kicked their way out of her mouth, stabbing her heart during their journey. Loudly, she cried like a newborn in need of feeding, a toddler who lost her mother in a toy store, and a woman left incomplete after losing her love.

The unbearable reality smashing inside her soul made her in dire need of relief. So she banged her head into the metal. She flung her back into the parapet. The additional pain added to her nightmare.

"Make it stop, make it stop, make it stop," she muttered.

When the pain in her heart didn't subside, she banged her head harder until the bar shook and rattled.

"Make it stop, make it stop."

The piercing pain circling the back of her head climbed her pain threshold and grew stronger with every hit. Blood tumbled down her neck and seeped into the collar of her shirt.

"Make it stop, make it stop, make it stop."

That's all Renee said, all that she could say, because the pain her heart was undergoing was causing the rest of her body to malfunction. No longer strong enough to continue with the self-harm, Renee lay on the ground, curled in the fetal position, where she lay in a puddle of glass and cried.

Chapter 1

Naked trees and cracked concrete under a shivering cold bed of snow dressed New York in misery. The rope of lights swirling around the Christmas tree reflected off the window Renee peered out of. Her view was limited, but she didn't need to see far and wide to know that on the night of Christmas Eve, people around the world were reveling in the holiday spirit. As her eyes roamed the beautifully lit homes stationed on Long Island, tears descended from the corners of her eyes. There were so many houses, yet none of them in her sight contained Julian. And because reality had set in on a holiday filled with joy, her heart ached and her world crumbled.

"Renee, come open your gift." The rainbow lights decorating the living room bounced off Dane's black shades. Behind their lenses, turmoil plagued her soul and sucked her dry. Life lost its meaning when her baby sister Reagan was murdered, an innocent pawn used in Carmen's game. Still, she displayed a calm exterior intended to soothe both her husband and her best friend. She was tired of the constant sympathy thrown her way, so in the presence of others, she played the role of a magician and created the illusion that all was well. However, it was only behind the shades that she could pretend. Without their barricade, her cover was blown and her emotions were exposed.

"Just leave it under the tree," Renee mumbled.

"Renee, come open your gift. We have every other day of the year to be depressed, so let's not make today one of them."

It was shocking to hear Metro's voice. He hadn't uttered a word to Renee since she left Julian and Manhattan. Part of her wondered if she'd disappointed him too, if he too blamed her for Reagan's death like she knew in her heart Dane had. If it weren't for Renee bringing Carmen into their world, Reagan would still be alive, and their circle still intact. A rainforest of tears flooded Renee's cheeks. With every fiber of her being, she wanted to remain where she stood and not move an inch, but she no longer had the luxury and flexibility to be disobedient and hardheaded—not without consequences. Dane and Metro were all she had left, and if she drove them away, life would officially be over.

With the back of her hand, Renee erased her tears. She did as she was told. She sat Indian-style on the floor in front of the couple. Dane held a small, neatly wrapped silver box in her outstretched hand. After what felt like hours of admiring the box, Renee finally accepted it. It was extremely light and made her question its contents. She opened it and was puzzled to find merely a folded piece of paper in the center of its four walls. She immediately began to unfold the note. There was an address written in black ink.

"What is this?" Renee turned the paper over, searching for a clue.

"It's Julian's address," Dane confessed.

Renee's entire body became numb, and a vivid memory of her standing in her Manhattan living room, listening to Tina's phone recording, dominated her thoughts and pushed her back into the past.

"Renee!"

Dane's call snatched Renee out of her thoughts. She stared at Dane with wide eyes, her face smothered with shock. As if Dane had suddenly become a stranger, Renee questioned whether she was friend or foe. The vacant look in Renee's eyes confirmed the emptiness and hollow feeling in the pit of her heart.

Dane waited for Renee's breathing to stabilize and her eyes to lower. For a while, they all sat, waiting for a verbal response. Instead, Renee sat on the carpet, rubbing the paper. That address stirred up so many emotions. Her stomach grew angry, and her vision started to cloud. What was she supposed to do with that address? Run into his arms and forget all about the past? Or was she supposed to turn that house into a box of ashes like she had her uncle Lyfe's, who choose Carmen over her?

She trapped the paper in the palm of her hand and allowed her fingers to act as its prison bars. Renee came to her feet and headed right back over to the window. She looked across the street at her neighbor's home. Their brick house was dipped in lights, but the glow and twinkle it gave off emulated love. That house was the perfect home. It was where children grew up and parents grew old. It was predictable and normal. It was safe.

Lost in its appearance, she created a family of her own. She imagined herself with Julian in the master bedroom, buried under the covers while play fighting and sharing multiple laughs, their children scattered around the house without a care in the world, enjoying the newest electronics to hit the market. Life was good. It replaced all that she had ever known and wished to forget. Yet, while she was active in a place of make-believe, her hand had crushed the address, and the paper scraped against her skin. The feeling of that white piece of paper stabbing into her whispered to Renee that that was not her home. And no matter how many times she wished upon a star and created a new life in her head, her current situation would remain and never just disappear into thin air.

She released the paper from her grasp and let go of her hopes and dreams.

"I don't know why you're showing me this, or what you intend for this to change, but that page of my life"—she pointed to the crumpled piece of paper on the floor—"is dead to me."

She gave the house across the street one last look and said her goodbyes. She forced her fragile frame to move. Weeks of stress ate away at her body and transformed the queen of New York into a weak-looking has-been. It was only a matter of time until her mental state plummeted into a state of oblivion and turned her into the boogeyman who came out in the day and terrorized anyone who got in her way. She looked at Dane, the Christmas tree's lights coloring her face red and green.

"Fuck with him if you want to, but don't expect me to help clean up whatever mess that traitor gets you into."

Renee prepared to make her exit. This was not a conversation she was willing to have. Dane intervening in her personal life irritated her. All she wanted was to be left alone while she dealt with the loss of her love in her own way, in her own time.

"Do nothing and you're dethroned," Metro warned.

Renee turned around, her head shaking and shoulders rising, all while giving a smirk.

"Life doesn't work that way for you anymore. You gave up your voice when you handed your business over to me." Renee pointed at Metro then at herself. She could feel the frustration creeping farther up her spine, and still, she stood firm, blocking any additional emotion trying to seep through.

"My connect, my army, my empire, my call!" Metro reminded her.

"Then it will be your demise," Renee spewed. Time slowed, and the air thickened. Giving up her power could never happen. So much had been stolen from her up until this time, and now Metro was threatening her? The building blocks that once held up a strong friendship at that second collapsed and caused dust so heavy to rise, no one could see clearly. Metro's finger inched its way into her face.

"Threats mean nothing coming from a has-been. Take what you brought to the table and leave!" Metro demanded.

"Go to hell!" Renee's hand flew up and smacked Metro's antagonizing finger out of her face. However, the action was answered with Metro's heavy hand meeting her right cheek.

Renee's small frame landed against her coffee table, her arm acting as a cushion an instant before hitting her head against the wood. Ringing ears and blurred vision temporarily tapped her out of the fight and left her disabled. Wide-eyed, she forced herself to focus, and that was when her hand opened the small side drawer built inside the table. It was one of the many homes where her firearms resided inside of her living room. Renee pointed her gun at Metro. It exploded, one time, two times, and finally three.

No one spoke a word. They all listened to the mechanical sounds of Santa moving around in his sleigh and Rudolph taking flight from the neighbor's roof. The decorations' movements pounded inside Metro's ears while he lay on the floor, his hand fighting to push the blood back into his body.

"I'm not stepping down," Renee growled. Her eyes twitched, and her conscience pushed her to shoot again, instructing her to hit his heart instead of the shoulder now soaked in blood. "I'm not stepping down," she repeated with her finger pressing down on the trigger when she blacked out.

Chapter 2

One leg hung beneath the porch swing's blanket, swinging back and forth. Snow falling from the sky touched down on Long Island's soul. Vodka and cranberry parted Renee's lips, a faint chuckle escaping her voice box before swallowing the liquid.

"They think I'm out," she mumbled. "They think I'm really out." Renee chuckled. Her laughter was uneven, uncomfortable, and on edge. "Tried to mourn a fuckin' breakup before I go on a murdering spree, and I get treated like a sack of shit." Renee's lips curled. "I always planned on burying that bitch Carmen for fucking Julian and killing Dane's sister. I just needed some time to heal. Now a whole bunch of new shit is in play." She pushed out cold air. "Now everything has to change, everything and anything. I'll make sure of that."

The knot on the back of Renee's head bulged out, the pulsating pain increasing with every individual chuckle. She tried to ignore the migraine it gave birth to and tough it out, but she knew eventually she'd need to use the ice pack and aspirin sitting beside her. Laughing some more after thinking about being caught off guard and hit by Dane, Renee finished her drink and poured herself a glass of vodka. Unscrewing the top of the bottle of aspirin, she swallowed a pill. The glass of poison followed behind the painkillers just moments before she snatched the ice pack from its seat and placed it on her head. The contact between her head and the ice was painful.

Renee took a deep breath and closed her eyes. *This can't be happening.* Her relationship with Dane and Metro was deteriorating, if not already dead. Hard changes were taking place with the two who were more like family than those who shared her DNA. However, the one thing that poked at her the most and ignited her anger was her inability to decipher which was worse— Metro taking away a life of power he'd given her, all while being fully aware she had been stripped of her body and respect as a child, or Dane's failure to intervene.

Renee didn't know how long she was out for after being hit, but she vaguely remembered a comment made by Metro before he made his exit: "She's a liability, but only because she's family will I keep her alive and force her to learn." The snow increased its speed. The railings of her porch were now covered in white. The sweatsuit Renee wore and the blanket covering her legs barely did anything to protect her from the cold, but the heat brewing inside her made the weather bearable. Renee took the ice pack off her head. She had officially hit rock bottom. Only hours after her confrontation with Dane and Metro, the majority of her resources had already jumped ship. Renee had told herself that Metro no longer had the power to dictate her career, but now she realized that since he vouched for her, handed her everything, and had history with everyone he had introduced to her, he could decide such circumstances. She had lost family, love, and now her friends. All she had left was herself.

Renee's leg shook as her eyes welled with tears. Opening them, she opened the floodgates and relieved her hurt. She had sat on that swing for hours, trying to make sense of the night's events and convince herself that being dethroned was for the best. But everything she told herself in order to feel better didn't stick. It only went in one ear and out the other. No matter how much she tried to find peace in the situation, she knew she never would without getting them back. None of the allies she gained through Dane and Metro responded to her texts or phone calls. It looked like her well had gone dry and her road had come to an end.

The sound of snow crushing beneath tires grabbed Renee's attention. Her neighbors were home from what looked like a night of last-minute shopping. Mrs. Gibson stepped out of the car with two bags in her hands. Climbing out the car, her husband grabbed a few bags from the back seat, then took the bags his wife held. Renee stood from her swing, her boots kicking the blanket to the side, leaving only her sweatsuit to keep her warm. Walking as close as she could to the front of her home, her hands fell on the porch railing and sank into the snow. Looking at the couple, she thought of the love she was denied the instant she found out he had shared himself with another. Mrs. Gibson opened the door to their home, their children screaming with excitement at their arrival.

It was Mrs. Gibson who saw her first. She was closing the door with one of the children hanging off her when she noticed Renee leering her way. Thrilled to have a new neighbor she hoped to call a friend in the near future, she waved enthusiastically like a big kid.

"Hi, Renee! How are you?"

Happiness, openness, and a zest for life oozed from her voice. There was never a time Renee could recall her not being positive. What different worlds they lived in. Renee threw her hand up, giving only a weak hello. Happy to have gotten that much from her neighbor, Mrs. Gibson continued to speak.

"Maybe we can do lunch soon!"

Renee just stared, feeling like a circle trying to fit into a square, uncomfortable and out of place. Alone with no man and no power, Renee no longer wanted peace but to blow off steam by finishing what everyone else had started. When there was nothing left to lose, you lost your mind.

"Renee, are you okay? Do you need me to come over there?"

Mrs. Gibson's loud, agitating voice brought to Renee's attention that she hadn't responded. "Yes, I'm okay!" Renee replied.

"So what do you say? We should have lunch soon, maybe head into the city somewhere?" Mrs. Gibson prayed Renee would say yes. In her opinion, Long Island was boring, and making a new friend was exactly what she needed.

Renee replayed in her head the question she was asked. It had been a long time since she had been out in the open just because, and that was when it hit her. If she wanted revenge, she couldn't be Jordan and use Metro's connections. *"Take what you brought to the table and leave."* Metro's words echoed through her head. Renee smiled and nodded her head. Forcing out a half-decent, friendly tone, she shouted, "I would love that, Prue. Just tell me when!" *Goodbye, Jordan. Hello, Renee. It's time for you to flaunt your power.*

"You got this place together quick."

Standing in the middle of Carmen's new living room, her mother, Raquel, took in the drastic transformation performed within only a few weeks. The once-dull and spacious apartment was now spruced up with spring colors and edgy furniture. Each item meshed together nicely, all while taking on a life of its own. The decor screamed, "Carmen," but the numbers her new place represented didn't.

"I can't take all the credit. My interior designer did lend a hand."

Scanning every corner and floor panel, Carmen smiled with pride. If there was one thing she loved, it was spending money and starting fresh. Her budget was no longer what it had been. She was limited nowadays, being that she no longer had anyone to care for her financially. The money she had received in the past from her uncle Lyfe and her deceased ex, Benz, was put away.

"You did good. I always said you got your good taste from your father."

Raquel continued to admire the decor while Carmen fell back into a time when she learned about her father's second life. Raquel's mention of her father automatically made Carmen think of Renee and her escape from New York. She now felt like a wounded animal being hunted.

"So, what's next?"

Raquel sits down on couch with a glass of wine. Carmen took a seat beside her mother and forced the thoughts of her father and sister out of her personal space.

"I was thinking of getting some artwork. The walls are looking kinda plain," Carmen replied.

"I'm not talking about the apartment, Carmen. I'm referring to you. What are *you* going to do next? You spent your entire time here decorating this apartment. I know you didn't come back home to play designer, and I know you're running out of men to take care of you." Her eyes glanced over her youngest child's new outfit.

Baffled by her empty hand, Carmen stood up to retrieve a replacement. With her back turned to her mother, her eyes rolled to the back of her head. Raquel's interrogation made it difficult for her to pour her wine without wasting it.

"I've only been here for a few weeks, Ma. Can I get myself settled before conquering the big things?"

"Carmen, why are you here?"

"You know why I'm here. I'm trying to better myself, and in order for me to do so, I need to be in my comfort zone. I need to be home."

"But why?" Raquel inquired. "Why do you need to better yourself? What's changed?"

Raquel wasn't buying what Carmen was trying to sell. She knew since the day her daughter called to tell her she was coming home that there were missing pages to the story. Sure, it was possible for someone to want to grow within the security of a familiar place, but Carmen wasn't that someone. She was a manipulator and opportunist. Raquel knew this because she, too, was a master at getting what she wanted. She was the greatest deceiver of them all.

Letting out a faint chuckle, Carmen sat on the loveseat across from her mother. The distance was very much needed. "New York has inspired me. I want more for myself. Why is that so hard to believe?" Carmen lifted the crystal up to her lips.

"What did you get yourself into? What are you hiding from?" Raquel's eyes searched her daughter's for answers the minute she lowered her glass. The lies that seeped from her mouth, along with the defensive wall Carmen put up, were all too familiar.

It wasn't until the death of her children's father that Raquel stopped running from the world and hiding who she was. In her early twenties, she met Daniel. She had taken on the role of his mistress without giving a second thought to the lives that would be affected. Instead, she welcomed the luxuries that came with an uncommitted relationship. Raquel kept her distance from acquiring any responsibilities. Her goal was to live life to the fullest, and that was unattainable when rules and expectations were laid out in front of you. Raquel lived in the moment, carefree. And when she became pregnant with her first-born, Madison, she gave the child to her sister and continued on the selfish road she'd paved.

Carmen, on the other hand, had forced Raquel out of her world. Her birth had changed Raquel's perception a great deal, but it did not have any effect on her and Daniel's affair. By that time, she had mastered hiding their relationship from everyone, including his wife. Raquel managed to keep up the mischief until Daniel's death.

Carmen considered telling her mother the truth. Taking a big gulp of the alcohol, she imagined how it would feel to set her soul free and express how she had found out the truth about her parents' relationship and her queen-pin sister who had chased her back into Miami. Not to mention her resentment toward her mother for not fighting for her father. They could have been a full-time family had her mother not been so content with being the other woman. With a stare that could burn holes through her mother, Carmen told Raquel exactly what she had been holding back, and she wished her mouth would deliver the message.

Saved by the bell, Raquel's doorbell ringtone alerted her of an incoming call. Without looking at the screen, she picked up the phone with her eyes locked on her daughter, who wouldn't voice her honesty. "Priceless Realty, this is Raquel Hunt." Pausing, Raquel took in the voice on the other end and smiled. Her change of mood lightened up the tension. "Zeke, how are you, and how is that gorgeous home you recently purchased?"

Raquel made her way across the room, but not before grabbing her drink. She wandered around the lounging area, occasionally nodding her head. "Tell him to be at my office tomorrow at noon. If he's serious, he'll have a place in a secluded area by the next day. If not, tell him not to bother inquiring about my services again."

After a fast set of goodbyes, Raquel finished off the liquid, refilled her glass, and sat at the bar.

"The name Zeke sounds familiar. Who is he?" Carmen queried.

"Your cousin Zeke."

Carmen scanned her mental Rolodex and didn't stop until she reached the letter Z. "Zeke? Are you talking about Aunt—"

"Yes, my sister's son." Raquel cut Carmen off mid-sentence. *The sister I trusted to raise my first-born and who disappointed me by allowing my daughter to strip. The sister I haven't spoken to in years. Yeah, that sister.*

Raquel didn't even want to hear her sister's name, let alone speak it. So, for her to keep in contact with her nephew was eyebrow-raising.

"You haven't spoken with them in years, so why now?"

Raquel poured a fresh glass of vodka and pushed aside the wine. "He bought a place out here a few months ago and hired me as his Realtor. Now he's throwing some business my way."

Raquel's lips were pursed and her eyes low, an automatic sign that her dealings with her nephew went beyond their family name. Carmen smiled, her mother's careful choice of words entertaining the conversation. There was more to the story. There was no way she'd deal with her sister's son out of the goodness of her heart.

"What are you covering up?" Carmen asked, getting straight to the point rather than lurking around.

"Stay in your lane, little girl," her mother warned. She aimed her pointer finger Carmen's way while the remainder of her fingers held on to the glass. She placed the glass on the bar. Raquel fought to pull her eyes from her daughter, annoyed that she even had the gall to question her. "We have reservations at Royalties. Get ready, because I'm hungry, and I will not be here all day waiting for you," she snapped.

Raquel hopped off the barstool and headed to the restroom, mumbling on the way. Twenty-five years Carmen's senior, Raquel was an attractive, business-savvy woman who took the easy way out in life and was far from being green in achieving fast money. Gone were the days of settling as someone's mistress. Her new hustle paid much more.

Shaking off her mother's attitude, Carmen began to walk out of the room until her mother's phone pinged. The alert led Carmen over to the barstool Raquel had vacated. It had apparently slipped out of her mother's back pocket.

You're gonna tell me what you're up to, whether you want to or not. Carmen grabbed the phone and searched its contacts. The various tag-names logged into the cell phone belonging to a woman over the age of 40 raised red flags. Yes, it could have been business, but Carmen now realized things were never so simple when they pertained to her mother. Carmen took screenshots of all the contacts' information with tag-names and sent them to herself.

When she heard her mother heading down the hall and back in her direction, she deleted the history of every text she'd just forwarded to herself. Raquel's footsteps grew closer. They were so close there was no time to put the phone back on the cushion of the seat. Without hesitation, Carmen met Raquel at the living room's entrance and handed it to her.

"Here you go, Ms. Secretive. You left this." Carmen placed the device in her mother's hand and didn't bother to delay her trip to her bedroom.

"Damn right! And next time, stay out of my business until you're ready to tell me yours."

Carmen paid no mind to her mother. It was not what Carmen wanted to hear.

Chapter 3

Down in the basement of Dane's favorite abandoned Jersey home, she sat in a corner on top of dirt and small pieces of wood. Her back was hunched over, and her face was drained of color and emotion. With one leg outstretched and the other bent, her elbow rested on her knee as she finger-combed her hair. Her shades were trapped in her free hand, far from the red, puffy eyes they were meant to conceal.

"I'm not going to tell you where he is."

His voice cracked with every word. Short of breath, Fergus struggled to speak. Blood mixed with sweat coated his swollen face while the throbbing pain racing through his body forced his head to hang low. The inability to move due to being chained to a chair in a straitjacket sent him deeper into a place of discomfort.

Dane pushed her hair back and, for a few seconds, held on to a handful of strands before responding. "I know, but that's not why I'm keeping you around." Fergus's eyebrows rose, perspiration dripping from his hairline and landing on his legs. Dane had never seen Fergus so weak and would have never pictured her being the reason for his current state. She loved him and his deranged twin as much as she would have loved a child she birthed. She groomed them into the killers they were meant to be and took pride in their accomplishments. However, lies and betrayals could never be tolerated, never given a blind eye.

"I don't need you to tell me where your brother is. I'll find him. What I need to know is why you hid the fact that Jared is alive? Why have us all believe you cleaned him up?"

Fergus grinned, his eyes simultaneously opening and closing. He'd been tortured for days, beaten, and deprived of food, yet he refused to crack.

"Because you don't put the one you love in danger," crawled out.

Dane's leg dropped to the floor, a cloud of dust rising into the air. Her head flung backward, and a burst of laughter escaped from her mouth. The intensity of it resulted in her dropping her shades.

"And I always thought you were the smart one," she retorted.

Dane would have bet her last dime that if either of the twins had interrupted her business, it would have been Calloway, considering his ill temper and obscenely violent ways. But Fergus had blindsided her. She stood up and held on to the back of the chair Fergus was chained to. She bent down and spoke directly into his ear.

"There's no love in your future. It doesn't matter what team you bat for. That will always be one wish that will never come true."

Fergus was no Calloway. His heart was not completely black, and a small piece of normalcy still dwelled deep within his bloodstream. With a tensed face and blurred vision, Fergus tried to move. Her statement sent a type of discomfort that outweighed the chains and jacket. There were many things his dark soul could handle, including being ridiculed because of his homosexuality, but being told that love was not and could never be in his deck of cards was infuriating. With a tilt of the head, Fergus gave Dane his undivided attention.

"If a monster like you can find love, then anything is possible," he sneered.

Looking at one another, the two fell silent. *Monster,* echoed in each of their minds. It was statements like that that revealed the difference between Fergus and Calloway. Fergus looked down on Dane and called her a monster like it was a bad thing, but Calloway would have sung that word with joy to describe her.

"Now that's the problem. That one pinch of normal lodged in your soul still gives you hope that everything will one day be okay. I'm no bigger a monster than you. You've just fooled yourself into believing that I am."

"I would have had a chance at life if it weren't for you." Tears appeared in the corners of Fergus's eyes, and for the first time in life, he did nothing to stop them from falling.

Dane giggled. "Was that before or after you two killed your pervert uncle? Take responsibility for your choices. You're a killer. Your life was over way before I came into the picture."

This conversation between Dane and Fergus was long overdue. Although he never said a word regarding his thoughts about her, Dane always knew he took his child-hood hurt and frustration out on her, the only person who understood them and used their skills instead of rejecting them. Fergus believed Dane had only pulled him deeper into Dante's Inferno. It didn't matter if he took pleasure in his decision to kill. In his mind, he saw no fault in him and Calloway killing their abuser and everyone else they had murdered.

"I kill because I have to," he coolly confessed.

"You kill because you want to," Dane challenged.

The anger in Dane's voice was undeniable. Fergus sick-ened her to the core, and it wasn't until that very second that she picked up on the common sense he lacked.

"You and your gay-boy motherfuckin' blues. Is Jared even gay?" Part of Dane hoped he was, because at least all of this would make sense. When Fergus focused on the wall in front of him and didn't utter a word, Dane's last bit of hope dissolved with every second of silence. *Straight dick will get you killed,* skipped through her mind.

After minutes of Dane staring holes into the side of his face, Fergus finally spoke up. "Don't kill him. Let this end with me."

"As much as your betrayal for love inspires me, I could give two shits about what you have to say."

Dane rested her hands on his shoulders. Never had she imagined the twins would deceive her, but after coming to terms with the fact that Renee's loyalty was questionable, the brothers' deception was no longer surprising.

"Calloway . . . Please don't kill him." His voice jumped an octave. His selfish decision to save Jared called for his brother's life.

"I wish I didn't have to," Dane mumbled.

Closing his eyes, Fergus inhaled his last breath, filling his lungs with stale air. He prepared for its escape when his neck snapped and his introduction to death began. Crackling bones awakened the ghost of victims past and welcomed him to life after death. Life seeped out of Fergus's pores, and calmness engulfed the room as his body came to a standstill.

"Sleep well," Dane whispered, her hand rubbing his dirty brown hair. His pale white skin was clammy.

A sea of memories flashed before Dane's eyes. Balling her free hand into a fist, Dane fought to go back in time to when she first met Fergus and Calloway. They were bloody, starved, and determined to rid the earth of their uncle's body. They were in need of her assistance, and she helped them dispose of the corpse and later took them under her wing. The memories were remarkable, but no matter how much she wished that she could go back in time and warn them of their future errors, she couldn't.

Devastation overcame her. She shoved Fergus's body, causing his chair to topple over. The instant he met the floor, so did she. All of her soldiers were crumbling, and her new reality became too much to bear. After days of holding in sobs, she finally let them escape. Her screams were loud enough to crack mirrors, and her aggression was strong enough to move mountains. Her vision became blurry, and all self-control was thrown out the window. What saved her psyche from going over the edge was the sound of a text hitting Fergus's phone. With makeup dripping and adrenaline pumping, she moved toward Fergus and retrieved the phone. The sight of Calloway's name pulled her back into a world of sanity.

Fergus, we need to meet up. How much longer will Dane be needing you, and why haven't I been recruited?

While she wiped tears from her face, cosmetics stained her fingers, and a wicked smile appeared. Because I want you to die alone, Dane replied. She immediately followed up with another text.

You crossed me. Now deal with the consequences.

Dane dropped the phone, and it landed beside Fergus's lifeless body. Before making her exit, she slowly walked around the space, admiring her place of doom one last time. Many lives ended here, and the thoughts alone soothed her soul.

Stepping outside the city's eyesore, she gave it one last look. A weak smile made an appearance.

"Blow it up!" she hollered. The wind carried her voice into the ears of her husband.

Dane jumped inside her car, sank her head into the headrest, and closed her eyes. Life was getting to her, and she needed to regroup. Minutes later, there was a loud explosion, and the smell of smoke raided her nostrils. This was war, and her first attack was leaving Calloway without his brother and no body to bury.

Chapter 4

Debris and ash were the only remains from the fire. New Jersey's eyesore was now nonexistent and had left a gap in the middle of the state. Its disappearance brought Dane's words to life and confirmed his brother's death. Never would the house fall unless a point was being made. This symbolized the end of an era and a business relationship made in heaven. Calloway kept a secret he should have told Dane, a secret that, when revealed, she could not overlook. His eyes bugged out and his body shook. He wanted to turn over burned wood and kick aside garbage in search of his twin, but his legs wouldn't budge.

The news had already informed American viewers that the only human remains discovered at the site were teeth and toes. Dane was toying with him. She had left evidence behind that Fergus had died in that very place, but she made the whereabouts of his corpse forever a mystery. Allowing Calloway to bury his brother would have been too nice, so she left him with nothing but a hole in the middle of dirt for Calloway to find comfort in.

Looking at the destruction in awe, Calloway mumbled frivolous things until finally forming a comprehensive sentence.

"She really did it. She really did it," he repeated.

Maneuvering his head from left to right, Calloway couldn't believe what Dane had done. In the pit of his soul, he knew she killed Fergus, but still, he held on to denial. After working all those years under Dane, he had believed that he and his brother were exempt from her wrath. The guidance she supplied them was a barrier he assumed not even she could puncture.

"She really did it."

The echo of footsteps kicking through rubble blared in Calloway's ears and sent him into a deep, dark place he only visited when devastated with pain.

"What else did he say to you?" Calloway growled. He turned his face to the side just enough for him to see cream-colored boots plunged in the snow.

"I told you," the voice replied with annoyance and aggression festering in every word.

"Tell me again!" Calloway yelled. Not only was he hurt, but he was disgusted that, for the first time in life, he needed someone other than his brother. However, the person he needed to help take down Dane mirrored his own life, and that was a problem. They were too similar, and what irked him to the bone was, instead of this man fearing Calloway, he understood him.

Silence swept over the cold and gloomy New Jersey. Breathing quickly in and out, Calloway fought to repeat himself. "Just tell me what he said."

After minutes of brutal silence, his new partner finally spoke. "He told me Dane knew and that if I didn't hear from you or him within forty-eight hours, to kill them all."

"Now, why the fuck would he think you would listen to him? Were you two fuckin' or something?"

Calloway knew the answer to his question but needed to throw swords at whoever was around. He was upset with Fergus's heart placing them in this situation and wished it died right along with his own, so for the time being, he needed a punching bag.

"You're funny, but you know what would be funnier? Killing you where I'm sure she gutted Fergus."

Five feet from where Calloway stood, his new partner in crime slammed his foot repeatedly in the ground, creating a miniature ditch. "I bet it happened right here. Come join him, Calloway," he urged.

Patience evaporated into the air, and snowflakes the size of cotton balls descended to earth. With cheeks beaming red and the bottom of his slacks stained with snow, Calloway rushed forward, the clutter on the ground slightly slowing him down. He flung his arms out in front of him, his hands landing inches from the disrespectful man's neck. However, before his hands could wrap around his neck and cut off his air supply, he froze in place. His feet pushed up dirt while he stared down the barrel of a .45.

"One day you'll get your chance to try to kill me, but not today. Today we'll help each other take out Dane and everyone else in Renee's circle. That way, you get your revenge, and Renee will have no choice but to take me back once she's alone. Stick to the plan."

Jared aimed the gun directly at the middle of Calloway's temple. If it weren't for Fergus warning him that Renee knew he was still alive, he would have died the night Tina spilled the beans. Like a cat with nine lives, he had escaped death once again and, in the process, promised himself he wouldn't leave this earth until Renee was his. Jared still intended to capture her love and had planned to leave her with nothing in order for him to be her everything. The love he had for Renee had grown, and there was no indication that it would ever deflate.

Calloway slapped the gun out of his face. "It makes no sense that Fergus would contact you and not me," Calloway said. "He only texted me to say he'll be going out of town to handle some business with Dane." Calloway threw his hands behind his head, confusion surging through his veins.

"That's because he didn't have time to contact you. He probably sent me the text seconds before being kidnapped. She knows how you two operate, so she sent that text to you as a way of holding you off. It's a form of insurance so she could do whatever she wanted without you intervening."

Calloway slammed his arms down at his sides. "Then why not kill me too? Why not do it all at once?" Calloway should have known the answers to the questions rushing through his mind, but the stress and emotions filling his veins took away all knowledge of his mentor.

"Because you're the grand finale," Jared enlightened him.

"No, Renee's bitch of a sister Carmen is, not me!" Calloway declared, his index finger inches from Jared's face. His hand closed into a fist. He punched against his own chest. "Dane went crazy ever since that cunt killed her sister. She would still be in her right mind, and my brother would be alive if it weren't for her!"

Life was breaking Calloway down. He still searched for logical reasoning for Dane's actions, but he came up short. He crumbled inside over their broken friendship.

"I want her head. I want her gone," Calloway emphasized. Drool slithered out of the corners of his mouth. Like a savage, he craved the blood of Carmen—the culprit behind everyone's downfall.

"You said you wanted help with Dane. I agreed to help you with her and only her," Jared reminded him.

"Now agree to help with Carmen. Like Fergus told you, you owe us. Besides, if you do this, it will only make you look good in Renee's eyes. Carmen is a snake in need of skinning," he said, seething.

Staring at Calloway, Jared allowed his words to sink in and marinate. Carmen was a snake, a wannabe out for Renee's crown. Jared never did like her, and being reminded of Reagan's death only made the situation more intriguing. Carmen's demise would be the icing on the cake and the icebreaker for his and Renee's love.

"When will we take out Dane?" Jared asked.

"Soon, but first, we cut out the cancer."

Chapter 5

Rain tap-danced on the windowsills and seeped through the open kitchen window. Water trickled on the ceramic tiles and surged together to make one big puddle. He listened to the tranquil sounds of nature and welcomed their peace, but his mind was still in disarray. The clock in his head counted down the minutes to his mental breakdown. Suddenly, a monstrous laugh escaped from his chest and punched through his lips, the intensity of its sound matching the first bolt of lightning entering the sky.

"You're shittin' me, right? Tell me you're lying," Julian said. The laughter continued, all while shortness of breath kicked in.

Sitting in her chair sideways, Dane crossed her arms, and her face twisted upward. "Does it look like I'm joking?" she asked.

Dane's voice took on a tone of its own and clawed its way into Julian's eardrums. However, Julian ignored her coldness. "You have to be joking, because you did not just tell me that Renee now has nothing!" Julian screamed. His voice jumped high, and his fist banged low against the table.

Through her shades, Dane took in his act of aggression. "Bang again. I don't think your neighbors heard," she sarcastically replied.

"You're telling me Renee has nothing. What the fuck is wrong with you?"

Julian respected Dane. She and Metro had been in his and Renee's lives for many moons and turned them into millionaires. Yet buried somewhere deep inside, he always resented her for having a hand in the monster Renee had become. Money was nice, but the callous creature inside of Renee that Dane nurtured wasn't worth it. And now that Renee had reached her peak, Dane was letting her go and allowing her to roam freely around the city with no leash.

"It won't be forever. Just until she learns to kill those emotions of hers and remember what's important."

Dane looked over his place. It was a two-family Long Island home. A home Dane had a feeling belonged to Julian months before Renee kicked him out. Every necessity was available the second he moved in. Everything appeared well kept and had "home" written all over it.

"You're pushing her. You think you're teaching her a lesson, but really the tables will turn and blow up in your face. Don't test her," Julian warned. His words were sincere yet alarming. There was no one who knew Renee better than him, so if Dane had any sense, she would push her stubbornness to the side and listen.

"Nothing that I can't handle will happen. She'll come back once it's offered to her."

"How can you be so sure?" Julian challenged. "Can you really guarantee that after I broke her heart and you kicked her while she was down, she'll even want that type of life back? She'll want your friendship back?"

Behind the dark shades, Dane looked Julian in the eye and sat speechless, open to now acknowledging a newly created fear within her. After the death of Reagan, she was afraid of losing someone else close to her, and as a result of that fear, Dane gave Metro hell about clipping Renee's wings until he eventually agreed to let Renee back into her position after time had passed. Never had it crossed her mind that Renee would not want to come back.

Tight jawed, self-assured, and partly in denial, Dane replied by saying, "That won't happen."

Again, Julian laughed. "Dane, would you come back?"

His valid points and wall-cornering questions were enough to make Dane want to calm her nerves and pop a Valium. Her lack of response answered his questions and forced him to push out another.

"Since you can't answer that, then tell me this: what did she have to say about the note?"

Dane turned away. She had been defeated by his questions and needed to retreat so that she could go home and lick her wounds. "I didn't tell her."

Julian's body stiffened, and the color in his face disappeared. On that day, Dane was the bearer of bad news. There was nothing she had said during their meeting that was helpful.

"The timing was never right," was the only explanation she gave.

Julian had gone weeks without drinking. He needed a clear mind to figure out how he would get Renee back. However, the more he thought about fixing their relationship and repairing what was broken, the more he wondered if it was worth it. Being in a relationship with Renee wasn't easy, and whenever things seemed to look up, they fell apart right before his eyes. Renee didn't understand his feelings or where his faults came from, nor did she try to. So when she kicked him out the night she discovered he had slept with Carmen, Julian had a lot of time to rethink the relationship. Some days seemed dark and unbearable without her, and Julian felt himself suffocating a handful more with every morning he woke up. It had been those feelings that convinced him that their love was worth salvaging.

After hearing that Renee knew nothing about the letter Carmen had left behind before she retreated to Miami, the letter meant to inform Renee of the additional half-sister she knew nothing about her father creating, the burning liquid started to call him. There was too much going on too soon, and Julian would be a fool if he didn't succumb to liquor. He stood from the table and grabbed a bottle of scotch from the cabinet. He unscrewed the top, tossed it on the counter, and drank straight from the bottle. After three gulps of the warm brown, he sat back in his seat and slid the liquid over to Dane.

Dane had dropped the ball. She now realized she'd thrown Renee out and into a world where they didn't know whether Renee's mystery sister was friend or foe. Had this "sister," if she was real, been anything like Carmen, Renee would be unaware of this problem simply because Dane had failed to inform her. She grabbed the bottle without hesitation and finished it. She slammed the glass bottle down, its cracked sides threatening to pop.

"I'll tell her that when we went back to the house, we found the note Carmen had written."

Julian nodded, acknowledging everything Dane had said. Minutes turned to hours, and before Julian and Dane realized it, they were both laid out in the living room, drunk and rambling random things. Each was going through hard times and fought not to self-destruct, but it seemed like the more they fought, the harder things got.

"There was nothing I could do to get her to even talk to you. Nothing matters to her but what you've done," Dane slurred. On the floor, she spoke to Julian while looking up at the ceiling, unable to focus entirely. "You've fucked up."

Devastated and lost in a world of intoxication, Julian thought about his mistake and the damage he had caused.

His days were dark, and his heart was wrenching without Renee. Memories and pain ate away at his soul. It was a constantly recurring feeling, causing him to want her back. Taking a deep breath, now sure of his next move, Julian forced himself up from the couch.

"I want her back," he announced.

Dane wasn't listening. She was lost in her own whirlwind of problems. She paid him no mind until she heard him say, "Give me her address. I need to see her."

Chapter 6

People exited the double doors in a cheerful and entertained mood. Laughter was good for the soul, and it left tonight's audiences' faces hurting and in good spirits. Renee and Prue left the comedy club snickering while wiping the tears their laughter brought out. It was the second night that week the ladies had gone out together, and so far, all was well. Being normal looked good on Renee and kept her calm. However, there were times when her mind drifted off and reminded her she had revenge to obtain.

"How's the family?" Renee blurted out. The question came out rushed and shaky. Renee had no idea how to strike up a conversation with someone new. Her social interactions had been limited to her inner circle. For new people she had to converse with, once upon a time, she'd investigate and learn all there was to know about the individual. Living a dirty life required strategic planning, a skillset she'd lost once Julian broke her heart. Shortly after those secrets had come to light, Renee threw away her years of training and didn't bother researching her new neighbors.

Nothing mattered anymore except the mourning she was forced into. Julian had broken her, and with those shattered pieces came laziness. Now that she sat in her new position in life, she wished she'd done the work and brought fragments of her old life with her. There was nothing more awkward than conversations with strangers. She was now expected to socialize, and if there was one thing she didn't like at all, it was communicating with others. She preferred to be antisocial. There was comfort obtained when living in your own world, unbothered by the thoughts and voices of humans.

"Everyone's good. Roy's visiting family, so I'm looking forward to his return."

The women turned a corner, their destination the parking lot.

"So, you hired a babysitter for your children?"

Prue's eyebrow rose. "Girl, my kids are grown. As much as I do believe they sometimes need a sitter every now and then to keep them from the foolishness they're into, I have to accept that they are old enough to take care of themselves."

Confused, Renee's mind shifted back to the little ones who had greeted Prue and Roy at the door. "Those kids at your house looked around eight or nine years old."

Prue smiled, the confusion now clarified. "Kyra and Davis are my grandkids. They're my son's children. I had them over for Christmas this year."

Renee nodded her head. "So how many kids do you have?" Renee found it easier to communicate by asking questions. It seemed to make the conversation flow and stay away from her.

"My son is twenty-two, and my daughter is twenty-eight," Prue answered proudly.

"You must be a good grandmother, because I can count on my fingers the number of times my grandparents spent the holidays with me." Renee hadn't planned on disclosing any information about herself that night, but just like that, something spilled out.

For the first time in a long time, Renee's mother, Janet, came to mind. Janet's parents were not active in Renee's life. Her grandparents on her father's side saw Renee as much as Janet allowed, but that ended completely when Renee's father, Daniel, passed.

"I love my grandbabies. I can't imagine not being around them for the holidays. It just pissed me off that this year my son had to go out of town. All they wanted was a white Christmas with their father, and he's still not home. The kids are with their mother now."

Prue became quiet. Her thoughts were focused on her kids and the fact that they were going nowhere fast. She zoned out, her eyes concentrating on what was in front of her. Renee allowed Prue to have her moment. She knew a blank stare filled with thoughts when she saw it. However, in a few minutes, her questioning would continue. From across the street, Prue always appeared to be well put together, so to see her unravel made Renee want to learn her secrets and what made her tick. Could it be, like in her own life, Prue was plagued with trouble? Slowly, Renee was easing into her comfort zone, where she was in charge and Prue was but a peasant placed in her presence for entertainment.

"Why wasn't he with his kids? Is your kid one of those who makes them but won't raise them?"

The women stopped. Cars conquered the streets and forced them to wait until they passed.

"Worse," Prue said. "He's a fuckin' criminal," she vomited.

The cheerful, happy-go-lucky Prudence was kicked out the door and replaced with honesty. Her need for friendship not only revolved around having a girls' night out, but having a friend she could speak with concerning her anything-but-perfect lifestyle and personality. The stress she had throughout the years caused her to turn to anti-depressants. The pills helped to temporarily resolve her inner issues, but what she needed the most was for her children to walk the straight and narrow and her thirst for money to be quenched.

Hearing the word "criminal" brought a sense of comfort to Renee, and her ears raised like a rabbit's. Her trying to fit in ceased, and Prue was now lured into her world.

"What kind of criminal is he? You make him sound like the bottom-of-the-barrel type."

"Because he is. He's a fuckin' drug dealer," she hissed. "Every day, he puts his life and freedom at stake for a few measly dollars. All Roy and I do is argue with him to leave it all alone, but he never does. All he says is he'll leave when he reaches his goal." She shook her head. "He talks the typical TV gangsta shit. 'Just a few moves and I'm out!'" Her voice changed in her attempt at mimicking a man.

Pain-filled tears rushed down her face. Prue fought to keep her composure, but there was just so much she could hold internally. Her eyes wandered around, and her feet constantly slammed against the ground while they waited for the green light to shine. Prue pushed the tears and her dreadlocks away after finally being granted access to walk across the street.

"I'm sorry. I just have so much anger inside. I guess I exploded." She cleared her throat and wiped at her nose.

Prue's apology meant nothing to Renee. The only value their conversation held was the insight into her drug-peddling son's life and how Renee could use him to her advantage. *Ain't this some shit? Do I smell a new resource in my midst?* Renee pulled back the smile threating to shine.

"What's his goal?"

"Huh?" Prue dug her hand inside her purse now that her car was close in distance.

"You said he wouldn't get out until he reached his goal. What is his goal?"

Prue's hand ended its search for the keys. She looked at Renee, a frustrated, pissed-off glare landing her way. "What does it matter, Renee? What significance does his goal hold when your child's out there every day risking his life? Dirty money means nothing!" Prue's eyes twitched. She couldn't sell that lie even though she wanted to.

"Dirty money means everything when it's taking care of you." Renee paused, taking in Prue's reaction. In only a few words, she let her know that the life she was drowning in was the very thing that kept her happy. Renee could see when a person struggled with inner demons. She had too many of her own she was forced to fight not to notice the signs. "I never saw you or Roy head out to work in the morning. At first, I thought maybe you guys inherited money, hit the lotto, or even ran a successful business, because if I can be honest, you guys are living very comfortably. But you told me the other night that you and Roy retired, and you complained about the small amount in checks you two receive monthly." Renee laughed, her past assumptions obviously far from the truth. "So, your *criminal* of a son has to be the reason for your lavish lifestyle, isn't he?"

Renee nodded toward the new diamond bracelet she witnessed Roy grace Prue's wrist with the other night.

"Your son pays for everything while you two splurge on whatever money you guys once gained on your own. Why use your own green for bills and necessities when your criminal of a son can handle it, right?"

It was brilliant, a moment of nothing but pure observation and strong concentration on Renee's end. Prue was concerned with her son's well-being and his choices in life, but the anger she was expressing was more along the lines of self-disappointment. Her greed was so strong she allowed her child to run the streets and remain in a danger zone. Yes, she argued with Zeke to get out, but that was just so she could say she tried and try to prove to the world, along with herself, that she was a good mother. But at the end of the day, she never rejected him taking care of her, and she never pushed as hard as she knew she should to get him out of that destructive lifestyle. Her greed was strong, and her heart was too lost in the land of money to give more effort than she already had to pull her son into the light.

Prue's eyes now sat on top of black goo created from mascara and eyeliner. The more she tried wiping her tears away, the messier it became. Zeke did promise that once he reached his goal, the drug world would be nothing but a memory lost in the past. He supplied his family with a good life and had to make sure they remained taken care of. A game of tug of war raged inside Prue, and she was allowing the bad, greedy side to win.

Prue chirped her car, and seconds later got inside. Grabbing a tissue, she asked Renee, "Why do you care? What is it to you that he's working toward a goal and I'm allowing him to for my own financial gain? What's your angle, you lay the guilt trip on me? No need. I do it every day of my life." For once, Prue spoke the truth pertaining to her and her son's ill doings.

Prue was a broken, horrible mother. However, Renee was a businesswoman, and when opportunity knocked, she opened the door and told it to take a seat.

"Have him work for me. He'll reach his goal sooner than he thinks, and this lifestyle you love so much will be guaranteed forever." Not too long before Renee agreed to mingle with Prue, she had nothing, and now by pure luck, her nothing turned to something.

Chapter 7

Watching the sunset was a beautiful thing. It was an indication that the day was coming to an end and people should slow down their pace. The vibe Miami gave off was nothing like New York's. It offered tranquility and second chances that Carmen could only hope for in the concrete jungle. A gush of wind blew her way and pushed her hair into her face. The smell of coconut and pineapple shampoo whisked its scent into her nostrils. This was the life, the peace it provided and negativity she escaped. However, this was a temporary fix. A bandage placed on a wound that should have been stitched up. Her abandoning the big city pushed her five steps back from where she originally wanted to be, but there was no looking back now. There was no remote control that could rewind time or undo the damage. It was much too late for that.

Now she sat back at square one and in need of a bulletproof plan that would land her out of harm's way and place Renee in a casket. Carmen knew flying out to Miami was a knee-jerk reaction, a fight-or-flight type of reaction that should have been thought over, but there was no time to think. Her life was at stake, and dying was not an option. The waves bashing against the rocks were heard from her twelfth-floor apartment. Their intense force reminded her of the bounty she imagined was placed on her head. She was sure Renee had released each and every one of her workers to track her down. So, like a sitting duck, she sat defenseless in the very state

Renee was bound to search first. It no longer mattered how Renee found out about her true intentions. What mattered was that she was coming for her, and Carmen was defenseless.

The death of the men in Carmen's life struck her hard. Instead of regrouping and going for the jugular, she used this time to mourn and accept defeat. Yet there was only so much mourning she could do before making a move.

The chirping of multiple birds echoing from her phone grabbed Carmen's attention and forced her to pick up the cell phone. She had a new text message.

If the boss gives the green light, then I'll roll.

That was the fifth text that Carmen had received in the past three days, and each time, she had received the exact message. It didn't take a rocket scientist to figure out that the numerous names in her mother's cell phone were convicts she had sold real estate to. Raquel was great at selling property to people who needed things done illegally, and those were the types of people Carmen needed now to help her. This was the very reason Carmen went cheap on her apartment. In the back of her mind, she knew building an army would cost money, so she had to have the funds. Her home was nice, but it wasn't the high standard she was used to.

These repetitive texts led Carmen to realize she should have reached out to her cousin first, but the fear of him waving her off was paralyzing and discouraging. She hoped his men were open for business without their boss's consent, yet according to the responses, she knew they were loyal. It didn't matter what she wrote. They wouldn't budge.

Annoyed that she was unable to talk her way into receiving a new crew without the hassle of getting permission, she dropped her head back into the chair, both hands squeezing her smartphone. It was her way of letting her frustration out in the absence of her stress ball. After losing her strength, she took a deep breath and scrolled down to Zeke's name. Pushing aside her fears and one-track mind of doing everything the fast way, she texted, This is Carmen, Raquel's daughter. I have a business proposition for you.

She sent the message, dropped the cell phone on the table, and closed her eyes. She didn't expect an instant response, so she used the time she had to take advantage of the peace she probably would miss out on after striking back at Renee.

Ten minutes later, her phone went off. Her left eye opened. *Fast response.*

She retrieved her phone from the miniature glass table nearby. You have a lot to learn, cuz. Meet me at this address tomorrow night at eleven.

An address of a lounge on the west side followed the message. Closing out the text, Carmen tossed the phone back on the table. Preparing to sleep outside on the terrace, she pulled the blanket up to her shoulders and shifted in the chair until comfort was attained. Drifting off to a land where dreams dwelled and mankind reenergized, one last thought entered her mind.

At least he didn't say no.

Dressed to head out on the streets of Miami brought back many memories. Carmen was no longer in the same place she was when she first lived in Florida. Her mindset had changed, and her need for independence was now a priority. Some nights in bed, she wanted to cry and release all the aggression and agony she had decaying inside. She questioned whether it was all worth it, but like the night she turned over those three pictures in her destroyed kitchen, she refused to give Renee the satisfaction of knowing she had her distraught and, honestly, nervous.

Although it was no longer of importance, Carmen did wonder from time to time how Renee had figured out her true intentions so quickly. Yet every time the question came to mind, Carmen reminded herself that what mattered was Renee trying to tear Carmen's life apart in order to show her who was queen. Facts such as that kept Carmen focused and sharp.

Popping the cap off her eyeliner, Carmen went for the bottom of her eye, then dropped the pencil in the sink when her fingers could no longer support the makeup. The constant hand shaking resulted in her releasing the black pencil and looking in the mirror at the woman staring back at her. She looked stressed, tired, and unsure, all in one gaze. The darkness under her eyes was a result of many sleepless nights, and now like many other times, she wondered if she was in over her head. Knowing the answer to her own question, Carmen snatched the pencil from the basin and effortlessly added makeup to her tired-looking eyes. This world she had entered was eating her alive, but instead of making an exit, she aimed to see it through and hoped for success.

One Hour Later

A handful of people sat scattered around the stuffy, dimly lit lounge, drained of any energy. The boards that covered the windows eliminated outside light while trapping inside foul smells of mildew and sweat. The stench assaulted newcomers, violating them as they stepped farther inside without protest. A small number of individuals smoked, swallowing nicotine residue as they stained their lips with beer or brandy.

Slowly, the heavy metal door slammed shut behind Carmen, her prism heels stabbing into cigarette butts and condom wrappers. This was not the Miami she remembered, not the lounges she remembered littering its sidewalks and supplying entertainment. No, this was a downgrade, a depression many tried to avoid. This was Miami's underworld. The cheap cancer sticks burned off smoke that led Carmen directly where she needed to go. It was a ghost town in that place. No one bothered to look her way, and instead, they focused on their imaginations playing tricks on them. They visualized snow and places of happiness they had yet to see. They pictured life outside of these four walls.

In the back of the first floor, Carmen opened a door leading downstairs. Flashbacks of entering Benz's basement made her slam her eyes shut. Stuck at the top of the stairs, she found it in her to shake off her emotions and push forward. Downstairs offered a room where sectional sofas outlined its walls. The carpeted floor had small burned holes in it, and the walls held up wood-framed photographs outlined with dust. However, the room was clean and comfortable enough for customers to leave their world and enter a drug-induced realm.

A large number of people occupied the hideout, and its tables sat infested with white powder. The looks on the customers' faces were dead and impassive. One by one, Carmen examined every face in the room until she landed on the last. His eyes told stories that seemed to never end, and although his left eye was without color and had lost sight a year ago, it still reeked of anger. Brown-skinned with a medium build, his upper body fell forward, and his baggy plaid shirt hung off his short arms.

Carmen walked to the far end of the sofa and pulled up a wooden chair. She waited for her cousin to speak, then decided to talk when he held on to silence.

"Thank you for meeting with me. There's an issue that I need taken care of, and of course, I'm willing to pay dearly for the muscle, but I need a team permanently afterward. Once the problem is handled, new territory will open in New York for me to claim, and I will need the manpower." Carmen paused, catching her breath. "Become my partner by supplying the muscle, and you'll get thirty percent."

Zeke didn't speak. In fact, when Carmen finished talking, she noticed he hadn't moved an inch. His expressionless glare and zero response sent uncomfortable vibes throughout her nervous system.

"You're disrespectful, and I don't like disrespectful people," he finally told her almost a full minute after she finished her speech.

Replaying her statement to him in her head, Carmen tried to pinpoint where she went wrong.

"You didn't ask me for permission to recruit my men. Instead, you went behind my back and contacted them directly. I must speak to your mother about giving out clients' information."

"My mother gave me nothing. I have my own way of getting information."

"Is that so?" Zeke antagonized her. "Then use those very same skills to get your own lackeys."

Zeke stood and placed his attention on a burly-looking man. He signaled for him to escort Carmen out.

"No!" Carmen's head violently shook from left to right between both men, her eyes jumping from the huge man to her cousin. "I'm sorry about that, but I'm desperate and need this shit taken care of like yesterday. Even though we're cousins, you don't know me from a hole in a wall. I took a chance going to your men first, because I thought if the money was right, they would move faster, opposed to the time it would take me to convince you to work with me."

Honesty leaked from Carmen's lips, but she never took her eyes off his lackey. She needed the reassurance that he wouldn't budge from his corner. She was at the end of her rope, and if Zeke didn't agree to work with her, she didn't know what she would do. Her life was on the clock, and it was only a matter of time until it struck midnight.

Zeke's one good eye burned holes through her face. From the first text she had sent his men, Zeke was alerted. He told them all what to say and the order they should respond in. Loyalty was the name of the game he played, and when you're selling drugs ranging from prescription pills to heroin, the mouths of people on the team needed to be shut. Zeke knew who Carmen was, and he sent her jumping through hoops until he took all of her options away and made himself her only escape route. "You're naive and messy. I would have thought, since you have the same blood running through your veins and have been on the arm of Benz, you would have learned something."

The moment Zeke's jeans reconnected with the couch cushions, his lackey stepped back into the darkness. Now assured she had Zeke's full attention, Carmen respired and continued with the meeting.

"How do you know about Benz?"

Zeke chuckled. "There goes that airheadedness again. When you're in this business, you need to know when a motherfucker eat, shit, and sleep. Benz was a heavyweight here in Miami, so when he went on hiatus, he left a door open for me to walk through with no interruptions. It's a shame what happened to him when he returned." He thought about the day he learned that Benz had been murdered. Seconds later, he shrugged it off.

"So, will you help me?"

"You're a liability, a rookie, and I shouldn't be associating with you, but on the strength of your mom's bougie ass doing business with me when I know she hates my mom, I'll help you." Zeke lit a cigarette, lifted his head up, and blew out smoke. "Who's giving you trouble?" he asked.

Carmen sat forward and scooted the chair closer to her cousin. She couldn't risk someone else hearing her next words. "Jordan. The head of New York."

Zeke dropped his head, alarmed. "You want me to take out the king of the streets? His ass owns some territory over here that no one's been able to touch since he declared it his, and the motherfucker isn't even stationed here." Zeke shook his head. He was having second thoughts concerning working with Carmen, who was handing him a suicide mission.

"Would it make you feel better if I told you your king is a queen?"

"What are you talking about?"

"You're afraid of a female, a broad who has you second-guessing taking over new territory. I may be a rookie, but I'm no coward." Carmen smiled, the power in the room shifting to her side.

"You're lying," Zeke hissed.

With her hands clasped in front of her and her elbows planted on her knees, Carmen broke it all down. "Her name is Renee, and she's my sister. Well, half-sister. I found out about her through our uncle. We share the same father. All of us." Carmen stopped, giving him the chance to think of Madison, the cousin she'd heard he actually communicated with. "My father was married to Renee's mother when he met Raquel. Their family is the reason mine never worked. I know the business, who she runs with, and where she's located. She was planning on retiring and handing everything over to me until she found out I had ulterior motives." Carmen paused and thought about the life Renee was living, the life she wanted. "Now she's after me, and I have to get her before she gets me."

"Fifty percent."

"What?"

"Fifty percent. You give me fifty once you take over New York. And the fee for me to take out Jordan just doubled."

Carmen fought not to protest. She realized her initial offer was an insult, considering the work that had to be put in.

"Fine." Carmen looked around, preparing to leave this depressing place when she noticed the outline of the lounge's past name before Zeke bought and renamed it. "What's the name of this place?" The lounge didn't scream crack house, but at the same time, it did. Zeke was right. She had a lot to learn.

"This place is Misery," he responded. "Misery Lounge, my high-class crack house."

The name said it all and spit the same kind of pain into his soul that it had hers.

Carmen nodded. "Contact me in two days for arrangements to be made. There will be no more waiting." She dropped the sunglasses planted on her head and covered her eyes. For some reason, she felt the dark lenses would shield her from this mind-numbing place named after Madison.

Chapter 8

In all the years they'd known each other, Julian and Dane had never spent this much time together on a consistent basis until now. The closest they came to spending this amount of time around each other was back in the day when Dane and Metro were teaching him and Renee the ins and outs of the business, grooming them to be their protégés. Now it was training day all over again. Except this time, Julian was learning things he hadn't learned before, and Renee wasn't by his side. Now that Renee was out of the picture, Julian was given all of her responsibilities, and the more Dane loaded on him, the more he felt they'd never let Renee back in.

"Now you know it all. Meeting with our connect was the last thing you needed to do." Dane focused on the road. It had been a long time since she had to introduce someone new to their connect. She always thought Renee would be the last.

"Dude's a fuckin' prick." Covering his eyes with his shades, Julian laid the passenger's seat back, preparing to rest his eyes.

Dane made a right turn down a residential block. Snow was barely visible on the sidewalks and streets. "I know, but he's loyal and has good shit, so Metro puts up with his ass."

Stopping at a light, Dane adjusted her rearview mirror when she saw a police car flashing its blue and red lights as its siren rang out while pulling up behind her.

"Pull over," the officer instructed over his PA system.

"Great," Dane mumbled. She pulled over to the right side of the road, took the keys out of the ignition, and put both of her hands on the steering wheel. Julian never moved. His lack of movement caused Dane to believe he had fallen asleep. "Julian, get up." Her eyes never left the rearview mirror. She watched as the white cop with dirty blond hair and sunburned skin, which she was sure he had obtained from traveling out of the country, approached her vehicle.

Julian looked behind him at the approaching cop. Not bothering to sit up, he lay back against his seat. "Those motherfuckers work for us. We'll be out of here ASAP." Julian closed his eyes.

Feeling uneasy, Dane spit out, "Something's not right." Every cop on their payroll knew her car, so what was this in reference to, and who was trying to capture a big fish?

Ignoring Dane's paranoia, Julian stayed quiet and relaxed. It wasn't long until the cop waltzed over to the driver's side and asked for Dane's license and registration without even bothering to bend down and look inside the car. Reaching into her glove compartment, Dane retrieved her information and handed it over to the stranger of a cop.

"May I ask what this is in reference to?" Dane inquired.

"No, you may not," the sunburned man answered. "Pop the trunk," he demanded, the palm of his hand slamming down on the roof of her ivory-colored Nissan Altima while he walked to the back of the car.

Dane looked over at Julian, who was now sitting up, surprised about what had just transpired between Dane and the cop. "What the fuck?" Julian voiced.

"Motherfucker didn't even look at me. This shit is a setup."

"Pop the trunk!" the cop screamed, the car vibrating from him banging on the back of the vehicle.

Dane's hand moved toward the car's hidden compartment for her gun when Julian redirected her. "Pop the
trunk," he advised. "I want to see something."

Going against her instincts, Dane popped the trunk.
Both she and Julian looked in the rearview mirror at the
cop fumbling around in the trunk and then tossing its
contents on the ground. Minutes later, he marched back
over to the driver's window.

"Step out of the vehicle slowly, and keep your hands
where I can see them."

"Why? Who the fuck sent you?" Dane yelled. After all of
her years of illegal activities, she refused to be put away
by a hot dog cop taking money under the table. Her mind
flipped through the endless amounts of pages of people
who'd have loved to see her behind bars.

The cop bent down. Now face-to-face with Dane, he
flashed a bag of heroin in front of her, an accomplished
smile across his face.

"Bullshit," Dane said, seething. "You planted that shit."

"Says the criminal," the cop chuckled.

Julian looked harder at the toy cop, his face jogging
his memory. "Officer Linksys, how are you on this fine
day?" Julian removed his shades, his confident and
intimidating smile lingering.

Officer Linksys's smile dropped. He stuffed the drugs
in his pocket and forced out a weak, "Julian, didn't see
you there."

"What is this all about, Linksys? What's with the bullshit?"

Linksys opened his mouth to speak, on the verge
of saying sentences riddled with fear and stuttering.
Julian continued speaking. "But before you answer that
question, tell me, how's the kids?"

In thirty-degree weather, beads of sweat blossomed on
Linksys's forehead. He swallowed and nodded, his eyes
frequently opening and closing. "They're good."

"Let's see a picture of them. You talk a lot about your kids, but you never showed me a picture of them." Julian was still smiling, his teeth never disappearing.

Breathing heavily, Linksys dug into his pocket and took out his wallet. Leaning over Dane, he handed it to Julian with a shaky hand.

Julian never looked at the picture. Instead, he gave the wallet to Dane. Looking at it, she took the photo out of its slot and tossed it into her glove compartment. She handed Linksys back his wallet.

"Linksys, this woman is a trained killer. She will kill your kids and you if you don't tell me what the fuck is going on."

Linksys thought about reaching for his gun, but when he looked into the eyes of Dane, something told him he wouldn't make it out alive. Caught between a rock and a hard place, Linksys wiped his forehead. "No bullshit, just doing what Jordan said to."

The car fell silent, and the anger both Julian and Dane wanted to release remained controlled.

"How come I don't know him?" Dane growled.

Julian thought over the situation before answering. "Because he's one of ours."

Grabbing hold of the steering wheel and squeezing it until her hands turned red, Dane constantly repeated her husband's words in her mind. *Take what you brought to the table and leave. Take what you brought to the table and leave.*

Unable to admit that she deserved the retaliation Renee was bringing her without the help of any of Dane's connections, Dane punched the steering wheel repeatedly and didn't stop until she was out of breath. "Dammit!" she let out. *She's not bowing down, not giving in!* Dane had underestimated Renee. She really thought she needed her in this cold, dark world. Catching her breath,

Dane composed herself. "I'm okay," she said to anyone who was listening. She laid her head back against the headrest and took one more deep breath. "Oh, who am I kidding?" Dane retrieved her gun faster than she ever had before and unloaded her clip into Linksys, who was still idling by her window. When he dropped, she pulled the gun back inside the car with her.

"Feel better now?" Julian asked.

"A little."

Chapter 9

Julian had to admit, he couldn't blame Renee for the stunt she had pulled. At first, he found her to be disgusting. Trying to get your mentor locked up was unforgettable. Then he thought hard about it. While Dane was ranting and raving on their way home, he started to not only justify to himself why Renee did what she did, but he started to understand it. He was the cause of it all, and no matter what Renee did, Julian felt incapable of passing judgment and forming anger. How could he? He had let her down and was the reason she had dropped her crown.

It was 11:58 a.m., and Julian was watching the time. Fully dressed, depressed, and stressed, he practiced trying to magically make the time jump to noon so that he wouldn't feel like an alcoholic drinking before twelve. Two agonizing minutes later, Julian unscrewed the cap of a bottle of vodka and poured himself a short glass full of the clear liquid. The liquor hadn't sat in the glass for ten seconds before he devoured it. The burning sensation brought him back to life and organized his thoughts. All he needed was a jump start, some vodka instead of OJ to kick-start his morning.

Violently shaking his head, Julian struggled between either welcoming or pushing away the burning sensation ripping through his chest. Eyes closed, Julian sat back on his sofa and decided to just let it be. Now at ease, because the voices in his head had finally come to a halt, Julian took the peaceful opportunity to plan his day out in his head. Keeping busy became a necessity because once you stopped moving, the whole world came crashing into you, forcing you to think of your issues. Mentally running down his to-do list, Julian was disappointed to discover that everything he needed to do had already been done, all except one thing.

Julian leaned over and momentarily placed his hands on his face. Ready to handle what he had been pushing off, Julian poured himself one more drink.

One for the road.

Less than twenty minutes later, he was on his way to Renee's. Taking the long way to Renee's, Julian questioned what he'd say to her when he finally saw her. Countless scenarios played in his mind, yet not one of them appealed to him enough for him to reenact. Feeling his brain on the verge of overloading with too many thoughts, he put down his window and allowed the winter's cold to ease his mind. Fifteen minutes into the drive, a barricade of roadblocks accompanied by police and crowds of people blocked him from making his next turn. Curious as to what could have transpired in the quiet suburban area, Julian pulled over and parked when he noticed all the attention was being placed on Iron Meds Pharmacy.

Reaching in his back seat, Julian grabbed his baseball hat and stuffed it on his head. Walking toward the mob of people with his head down, Julian pushed his way through until reaching the front of the crowd. There he witnessed police officers arresting staff and customers who could be seen at the business almost every day. Beside Julian was a young white man with missing teeth and scabs peppering his skin, no older than 25. He wore a winter coat with a hoodie underneath it, and franticly he tried scratching his arms through the heavy material.

"What's going on?" Julian asked, his head remaining down and his voice slightly disguised, his actions mimicking the addict's.

"It's a raid. Cops got an anonymous tip that Iron Meds been supplying more than just prescription drugs." The white boy sucked his teeth. "Shit! J and J only got two pharmacies they sell their shit out of. Now I gotta go to Brooklyn for my shit." Blowing out air, the guy walked away, pushing and shoving his way through the crowd.

From where Julian stood, he could see the cops tearing Iron Meds apart and leaving with his supply. The owner, Paul, was the last to be brought out of his pharmacy in handcuffs. His eyes landed on Julian before Julian walked away.

Five Hours Later

Pulling into her driveway, Renee saw a figure standing on her porch wearing black leather gloves, which gripped the ice-covered railing. Renee flashed her high beams and drove the darkness away from Julian's face. No one moved. They were stuck between the past and present, indecisive as to what time period they should fall into. Renee's heart told her to fall into the past and make it last, but her mind told her to live in the present where everything was evident.

With a simple punch of a button, Renee's garage door opened. She pulled into the dark and quiet space of her home and sat there, motionless. Her legs felt as heavy as cement. She sank her thick mane into the headrest and closed her eyes. Footsteps pierced her eardrums and caused her eyes to fly open. Her hand slowly dipped inside the armrest compartment. Her palm hugged the pistol while her pointer finger sat on the trigger.

The light tapping against the window pulled Renee from reckless thoughts and her firearm. With her weapon left inside its home, she turned to the window she didn't bother lowering. She just stared at the love of her life and observed all the changes in his appearance. Facial hair covered the lower half of his face, and his eyes reflected anger.

"Get out of the car," Julian demanded. His voice was as cold as the porch railing.

Renee didn't budge. She sat lost in the visual of him, a game of Ping-Pong transpiring within her heart where her emotions were the ball.

"Get out of the car!" he screamed. Julian wanted to make things right. He knew Renee well enough to know that she was resisting the inevitable. He didn't want a battle, only a resolution.

Yet the bass in his voice, along with a gush of wind seeping inside the car, chilled Renee to the bone. Renee's attention turned to the back of the car, where she noticed the garage door was still open. Julian pulled out his gun, the twin to the weapon that sat in Renee's armrest. He blew out the back window. Jamming his arm inside, he unlocked the door and jumped inside the vehicle. He leaned forward to unlock Renee's door before hopping back out. He flung her door open, grabbed her by the elbow, and led her into her home. After pushing her inside, he slammed his palm against the garage door button, granting them their much-needed privacy. Julian slammed the door behind him. She would speak with him whether she wanted to or not.

"We need to talk," he hissed. Julian was breathing hard, his heart racing and banging against his chest. Things had gone too far. He never intended for all of this to happen, but Renee had a way of pushing the calmest individual over the edge.

With a contorted face and a hurricane of thoughts, Renee remained silent. There were nights when she had books filled with things to tell Julian, and then there were times when her heart hurt so much, anguish seemed to wrap itself around her until she no longer had any air left to breathe. Even her words remained lodged in her throat. She wanted to vocalize her pain but couldn't.

Renee's eyes never strayed from Julian's. A light snicker leaked from the corners of her mouth. She was having fun watching him unravel, happy to see that he too was in pain. That one expression defeated all the hopes and dreams Julian had for them. Julian shook his head, disappointed in her insensitivity and unwillingness to communicate in order to make this right. Life was nothing but one big selfish game Renee didn't plan on bowing out of.

He looked around her home. His eyes settled on her dining room table, an imitation of the one he had purchased for her penthouse. Julian smirked. Renee insisted she could let go of anything and everything at the drop of a dime when really she held on until her hands became numb and fingers red. His smirk turned into a full-fledged loud, obnoxious laugh. He had finally seen the light, and suddenly all the anger he had for her resurfaced.

"You're a fucked-up, miserable woman." His laughter intensified. Losing his balance, he leaned against a wall for stability.

"Get the fuck out of my house," she snarled.

"No, really think about it," he begged, his laughter at an all-time high. "You have nothing, and still you insist on being alone. Still you insist on fighting. You can't fight the world alone, Renee. You just can't, no matter how many dirty cops you have, so grow the fuck up!"

Renee crossed her arms. "Grow up and do what, forgive you? You want me to run into your arms and tell you that I need you all because Metro decided to act like a kid and take his favorite toy known as New York away from me? If so, then you've lost your damn mind."

"I didn't know who she was, Renee!"

"It doesn't matter. None of it matters anymore."

Renee's eyes glanced at the staircase. She attempted to push past Julian, but her feet hit the brakes when he grabbed her arm and spun her in his direction. Their faces were so close that her hair slapped him in the face before landing on her shoulders.

"Do you forget what you put me through?"

Silence sealed Renee's lips.

"You kept yourself emotionally unavailable for years. You punished me, the only person who showed you unconditional love and lived with you in this depressing world known as your life. Never once did you take that into consideration. You only took it for granted."

Renee tried to free herself from his hold, but it only made Julian tighten his grip.

"You took my child from me," he reminded her.

Renee's entire being had gone numb, and the color in her face faded. Julian pushed her away from him, and the two stood in silence at the thought of their unborn child. Julian's eyes went from rage to agony, and slowly Renee came to grips with the underlying pain he endured. Only then did she consider how she might have contributed to his pain. From Julian sleeping with another woman to Renee sleeping with Jared, things were bound to explode in both their faces.

Renee slowly backed away from Julian. In that brief moment, she realized they both made mistakes.

Julian shook off the pain and allowed anger to lead their discussion when she didn't respond. He'd hoped that by visiting her, things would be different. Since they weren't, he'd jump to plan Z. "I know what you're trying to do, what you're going to do. Don't try building no shit in New York or Miami. Metro stripped you of those cities, not me. This shit is mine now, so keep your distance, or I'll hurt you more than I already have," Julian warned.

The threat was hard and disrespectful. It hurt Julian's soul to speak those words to her, but he needed her to hurt just like she had hurt him.

Leaving her speechless, he got into his car and punched the steering wheel multiple times until his strength dissolved and tiredness grabbed him. This was not what he wanted, but this was how Renee made it. So if this was what she wanted, Julian had to come to terms with the fact that he and Renee would never be.

Chapter 10

"Who the fuck are you?" Zeke stared down Calloway and Jared, who were standing in the middle of the lounge when he flicked the lights on. His lackey walked forward, his large frame standing out like a candle in a blackout.

"We want in." Calloway smiled.

"Congratulations, Ms. Melrose, you have just purchased a one-of-a-kind."

Raquel admired the two-floor glass building that sat on the street of South Beach. Its open space smelled of candy and flowers, fragrances spewing from Dane's and Raquel's bodies. Her voice carried to the second floor and back down.

Dane smiled. "Yes, this is a beautiful piece of property I have. Thank you for meeting me here this time of night. I just needed to give it one more look."

"I understand. If this were mine, I would come here every day just to stare at it." Raquel paused and looked around. "Forgive me, I know you mentioned it before, but what do you plan to use this space for? It has such potential and will go right with just about anything." Raquel folded her arms and walked across the floor, nodding her head at the architecture and delicate features.

"My jewelry store is expanding, and this will be my eye candy," Dane answered.

Raquel's feet terminated movement and turned in Dane's direction. "Perfect. You will certainly turn heads with this one. These glass walls and your collection of jewelry will give off magic for the store's outside appearance."

Raquel was impressed. She had done business with a lot of wealthy people, but Dane reeked of class, and her choice of wardrobe alone made her want to vomit with envy. Dane's glass-heeled stiletto boots and limited-edition glass clutch stole Raquel's attention. She fought not to inquire where Dane had made such purchases. Dane's presence secretly made Raquel feel inferior, but the foreign emotion would never rear its ugly head. In the world of Raquel, women came in second to her, but now that she shared a room with Dane, she had to remind herself of this constantly.

"You couldn't be more correct," Dane agreed. The effortless lie that rolled off her tongue was a tall tale created when needing a reason as to why her interest in the building existed. If the truth had been pulled from her mind and laid out on a table, Raquel would have discovered that the need for this property derived from a sentimental place and that a jewelry store was out of the equation. This was Reagan's dream, the graduation gift she was unable to receive due to her untimely death. Dane didn't know what she would do with this space. She had no hopes of opening a business, but she just knew she had to buy it for Reagan, even if she wasn't around to use it.

"What's the name of your company?" Raquel pried.

"Reagan's," Dane answered. Outside, four men were plastering newspapers on the spotless glass windows. Swiftly, they moved until no one could see inside unless they scaled the building.

Now on the other side of the room, Raquel's back faced Dane while she spoke. "A young lady by the name of Reagan was going to buy this place. Gorgeous girl. Then days after she told me she'd take it, I learned from the news that she was murdered in her home. Such a tragedy. I hope they catch the monster that did it. I didn't know her well, but she had such a great aura about her."

Raquel located her briefcase and took out a bottle of lotion to lather her hands. When she was done, she put it back and placed her bag on one of the two chairs in the room.

"They did," Dane told her.

As Raquel headed to the front of the room, her eyebrows jumped high. Her hands rubbed the vanilla-lily lotion deeper into her skin. "Really? I didn't hear about it."

"Yes. They got him rather quickly and learned that he had a partner. They haven't gotten her yet, but I have a feeling they will soon."

"Isn't that something? He'll turn over on whomever he was working with. They all do." Raquel noticed the newspaper covering the windows. "What are they doing?" She rushed to open the door.

"Relax, Ms. Hunt, they work for me. I'm a private person. The world doesn't need to see what sins I commit in here."

"Oh, okay. I understand." Raquel replayed the word "sins" in her mind. She found it odd that Dane would use that word, but she played along with it and laughed.

Dane's hand sat beside the light switch. "Would you roll over?"

"I don't follow you," Raquel confessed.

"Concerning the young girl who was murdered. You said that the murderer would turn over on his partner.

I'm asking, if you knew who the killer was, or their whereabouts for that matter, would you tell?"

Raquel did dirt she wouldn't speak of, but in order to close a deal, she believed in saying whatever she had to to keep the client happy. "Yes, most definitely!"

"I'm happy to hear that," Dane expressed.

Dane turned the lights off and, in just a few steps, made her way in front of Raquel. She wrapped her hand around her throat. Her pointy stiletto nails ripped into her neck and pierced her skin. Blood stained Dane's ivory-painted nails. Cutting off Raquel's breathing, Dane glared deep into her eyes.

"Where is your daughter?" Dane questioned. Her nails sank deeper into Raquel's flesh.

The piercing pain ricocheted throughout her body, and her loss of air caused her to hysterically move in an effort to maintain what air supply she had left. From left to right, Raquel moved her head, her hands pinching, scratching, and fumbling with Dane's in an attempt to be released from her hold. Her feet stomped down on the shoes she once admired. However, no movement or fight lured Dane away. Her stance was as solid as steel and never folded.

"That's not the answer I wanted to hear."

With her free hand, Dane grabbed Raquel's index finger and, with one swift move, broke it. Nails being dug into her neck mixed with a broken bone sent Raquel into a trance filled with pain. Cries screeched out of her, and tears dropped onto Dane's hand, sliding and plummeting to their death.

"This should have been easy. You said you would tell whatever you knew," Dane reminded her.

Looking back into Dane's eyes, Raquel saw vacant territory that ignited fear within her. There was no way she was leaving that building alive.

Dane loosened her hold just enough for Raquel to breathe. "Nothing's in your daughter's name, which means you played it smart. Wherever she is, I have a feeling you're responsible for putting her place in someone else's name. How did you know her past would come back to haunt her?"

Dane squeezed and rejected Raquel's lungs need for air. The thought of Carmen sickened her and sent her world red. With her healthy hand, Raquel scratched at Dane. The fight in her was quickly dissolving but still holding a little bit of power inside. It wasn't until she felt herself sliding into unconsciousness did she surrender. With the small amount of energy she held on to, Raquel nodded her head. That simple gesture was enough for Dane to loosen her hold. The second she did, Raquel's head fell to the side.

Carmen was her mother's daughter. Her need to be taken care of and constant moving around were clear indications that the apple hadn't fallen too far from the tree. When her daughter called and informed her that she was moving back home, she realized, Carmen was running from something and not just in need of bettering herself. Carmen asking for Raquel to find her an inexpensive home was a pure giveaway that something was wrong. So when Carmen arrived back home to Miami, Raquel made sure not to leave a paper trail as to her child's whereabouts. But now that death was likely to transpire, Raquel had no choice but to force Carmen to stand on her own two feet. Their deeds had come full circle, and now it was every woman for herself.

Looking at nothing in particular, Raquel allowed air to enter her lungs. Quickly, she tried sucking in all the air she could before she was deprived of it again. Her eyes rolled in the direction of Dane. She spoke slow and low. "Carmen is in an apartment two buildings down from my office. She's on the top floor."

"How did you know I was talking about Carmen?"

"Because at the end of the day, Madison only hurts herself and is bound to self-destruct. Besides, she's not important enough to make enemies."

"Then Carmen should have taken after her," Dane responded, her glower a combination of pain and destruction.

After using Raquel's neck to force her body to stand straight, Dane slid her free hand into her back pocket, where her switchblade was tucked. With the push of a button, the blade appeared. It wasn't out of its home for five seconds before it was lodged into Raquel's stomach. Dane pushed the blade down then up as far as Raquel's insides would allow, slashing her internal organs. Raquel's face emptied of any expression. Raquel's fingers drowned in blood from her dripping midsection and failed to reattach her broken skin. Staring Raquel in her eyes, Dane watched as every ounce of life that once filled her body seeped out within seconds.

Death was a funny thing. It was an unpredictable, memorable soul taker that robbed Dane of her humanity the day her parents passed. It was the reason she felt nothing while watching Raquel slip from the earth. Dane pushed the knife in deeper, turning it into a circle of motions, then pulling it out. Raquel's body dropped, Dane finally releasing her.

Snatching her clutch off the windowsill, Dane rammed her hand inside and pulled out a thin white handkerchief. She wiped the blood off the blade and dropped it on Raquel's body. Like water, its fabric took the form of waves and danced in the air until making a landing. The four men who plastered the windows with newspaper rushed into the venue. Two men held supplies equipped to rid the building of any evidence while the others concentrated on removing the body. Getting out of the workers' way, Dane was two seconds from the door when the middle-aged man wearing glasses and towering over Raquel stole her attention.

"She's not dead," he informed Dane. "To kill and dispose of her will be extra. You called for a cleanup. We did not—"

Dane walked over to the complaining man's partner and, without his permission, relieved him of the gun in his back pocket and shot Raquel in the skull. The unpredictable action silenced the man who spoke a mile a minute without bothering to take a breath. He and his crew watched Raquel's body jump, then relax. Their startled expressions roamed toward Dane.

"There, she's dead. Is there anything else?"

Motormouth did not ignore the fact that Dane still held on to the gun. He shook his head slowly, rendered speechless by Dane's cold-hearted execution.

"Good," she told him.

Dane wiped down the handle with the bottom of her blouse, allowed the gun to slip out of her hands, and walked out of the building. Standing in front of the exit, Dane wanted to turn around and look at the building once more. This was the one thing connecting her to Reagan, but she didn't turn around. If she had, she'd risk tears making an appearance, so she rushed out the door and hoped one day she'd return.

Dane was only three blocks away from her car. The moon lit her path as she walked down the streets while crying. Tears took over her face and made her a miniature ocean. However, no sobs escaped her mouth nor pain-filled expressions sat on her face. She'd cry because every now and then the action took her over. But she wouldn't let the world hear her pain, and she'd fight to minimize the agony her face showed.

Dane's cell phone rang, and she picked it up with the hand least stained with blood. "Hello."

"He came," Zeke informed. "Now what?"

"You play the part," she told him. "Put him on your team."

Chapter 11

From the back of the restaurant, Renee stood from the couch seated next to the crackling fire. Her fingers slid inside the diamond-encrusted brass-knuckle handle of her clutch purse. Once Renee stood to leave, Prue jumped up. Her red silk blouse stirred with each move she made while grabbing Renee's upper arm. Stopping in place, Renee looked at Prue's skinny fingers wrapped around her and gave her the nastiest snarl she could muster up. Prue withdrew her hold and began her plea.

"Just give him a few more minutes, please." Prue's eyes were wide and filled with desperation.

Renee ignored her pleas and walked away. Lateness was not only unacceptable but a deal-breaker.

Desperate and unwilling for her meal ticket to walk out the door, Prue ran after Renee and whispered in her ear, "You need him. If you didn't, you wouldn't have reached out."

The word "need" rarely, if ever, applied to Renee. She stopped in the center of the room, her mind trying to wrap itself around the fact that she did need him and she no longer had the necessities to be on top. She had to start from scratch and, therefore, could no longer be demanding.

"Five more minutes, and if he's not here . . ." Renee glared at Prue, leaving her to fill in the blank.

The two women took a seat while the front of the lounge filled with people who rolled their eyes and sucked their teeth at their seating. Three minutes later, a line of people marched into the room and quickly divided. The last to enter was Zeke and his henchman, who swiftly approached the women. Prue stood to greet her son and laid dirty looks on him. Zeke avoided her nonverbal reprimand, aware of his error.

"I apologize for being late. This is not how I normally conduct business," Zeke told Renee.

Still seated, Renee looked up at him and then turned the other way. Zeke took the opportunity to have a seat across from Renee. Renee looked forward and locked eyes with Jared, who was standing behind Zeke the entire time.

"Then it's settled. We're partners. Your beef is now my beef. In three months, after my team has proven themselves and you buy me out, they're all yours."

Although Zeke's outer appearance showed otherwise, internally he was doing backflips, ecstatic about not only working with Jordan but being that much closer to his retirement. For years he'd dreamed of walking away. And with the money Renee was offering to buy his team and operation, he met his retirement goal by far.

Zeke's original plan was to work with both Renee and Carmen and take everything their purses contained. He'd use his cousin's problems with her half-sister as a come-up and not a distraction. But Renee's money and reputation quickly changed his mind, making him see how great an ally she would be if ever needed. He'd take Carmen's cash, but his loyalty and manpower solely belonged to Renee, the bigger fish who wasn't blood. Giving Carmen access to the same crew Renee needed now sounded like suicide, and now that he sat across from the infamous Jordan, he had a feeling that she was not the sharing type. Yes, Carmen was blood. However, money was thicker in the game of greed.

Renee couldn't ignore Jared's presence throughout the meeting. He looked different, more demented, more . . . dangerous. During the entire meeting, the two stared at one another, ideas forming the more Renee looked at him.

They finalized the deal, and the meeting ended with handshakes and everyone going their separate ways. Jared walked across the street to the dark-colored vehicle in which Calloway sat behind the wheel. Once seated on the passenger's seat, Jared never got a chance to put his seat belt on before the back door opened and Renee got in. Calloway grimaced in the rearview mirror, pointing in Renee's direction.

"What are you doing here?" Calloway said, seething.

"I'm going with you two," Renee answered calmly, snapping her seat belt in place.

Calloway turned to Jared. "I don't know what the fuck you're trying to pull, but she's one of them."

"'Them' no longer exists," Renee replied. "Now 'us' is a completely different story." She knew nothing about Dane succeeding in killing Fergus, but for him to say "she's one of them" tipped her off that Dane was in hot water with him just like she was with her.

Jared turned around, his ears savoring the sound of a voice lost in time. Suddenly his anger over being rejected by Renee evaporated and his need for love bloomed. Calloway took off and, after minutes of driving, pulled onto a dead-end street. He pulled out his firearm and aimed it at Renee's forehead, the night's darkness a shadow over his face.

"Get the fuck out," he ordered. All Calloway visualized was Dane directing her to him. How she did it, he had no idea.

Thinking where he'd dump Renee's body, Calloway felt the tip of a cold gun pressed against the side of his temple. He didn't bother extracting his attention from Renee. Only one person was crazy enough to point a gun on him for a woman who ostracized him.

Renee smiled. The sight of Jared once again coming to her rescue confirmed she made the right move. Although it was hard to do, Calloway lowered his weapon.

Renee cleared her throat. "Business between Dane and me has been dismantled. I don't know what this is"—Renee's finger darted from one man to the other—"and I don't care, but it all changes now. I take it that you two now work for Zeke, which means you now work for me. So do what you do best, and keep me more untouchable than ever before."

Chapter 12

Cigarette smoke, perfume, and liquor swam through the atmosphere and created an unbearable stench that came across as stale and toxic. The loud music vibrating through the walls and floorboards was deafening and kept everyone stuck in a trance. Curls overlapped one another and bounced in the air as Madison walked off the stage. Her chest heaved in and out from the fast-paced song she was forced to keep up with in six-inch heels. Sweat dripped off her body and landed on the floor, mixing with the perspiration left behind by the last few dancers.

Sitting at her vanity table, Madison grabbed a package of baby wipes out of the top drawer and wiped down her face and underarms. Madison found a large piece of the mirror that hadn't been cracked and tidied herself up in it. A skinny brunette girl with freckles thrown on her cheeks flopped down at the vanity table beside her. Out of breath, she snatched off her top.

"Why do you insist on not using that shower? You're the only one allowed to use it, so you might as well stop trying to be like the rest of us."

Every time Nancy saw Madison, she reminded her that she was different and that the only reason she sat in the same boat as them was because she chose to.

"I step foot in that shower and that motherfucker Harry will think he owns me."

Madison tossed the used baby wipe in the trash and reapplied her lipstick and eyeliner. Her individuality shone through and, on countless occasions, made people question her attendance in such a place. Her boss, Harry, did whatever it took to keep her around and content. As the oldest dancer, she was the club's main attraction and had made a name for the place. This was all made possible when the club's top dancers left to work at a new high-tech club blocks away.

"Shit, then he can own me, because I'm trying to wash my ass right, and I'm not talking about these damn ho baths we've been doing."

Madison laughed. Nancy's foul mouth and outspoken personality made stripping easier. It made her feel like she was living a life where she was welcomed by her parents and stripped of her feelings of abandonment and depression, a life that wasn't a nightmare taking place in a strip club. Under the table, she played a game she called "break free." She struggled to pull the heel of her shoe from the sticky floor. Wasted liquor. Oftentimes, she too would indulge in drinking and getting high, but tonight she decided to let go of her drug dependency.

Nancy watched five girls with dark liquor filled to the brim of plastic cups blocking the door's entrance from her seat. Half of the club's employees occupied the makeup and locker room. A number of women scrambled to prepare their looks for their next set, while others took a breather and had idle conversations. Missing floor panels, locker doors hanging off their hinges, and cushions from inside the seats seeping out reminded the women there was no place like home and that they shouldn't be there to begin with. Nancy shook her head and sucked her teeth at the sight of the women. She wished one of them would ask what she was looking at just so she could tell them off.

"I can't stand those broads. Why the fuck didn't you beat their asses when they cracked your mirror?" Nancy inquired.

Like Madison, Nancy was intelligent and once had a bright future ahead of her. However, that changed the night of her best friend's bachelorette party. The group of friends celebrating their childhood friend jumping the broom had stumbled into the strip club Nancy now sat in, drunk and full of energy. It didn't matter that the club only employed female strippers. They wanted to party, and since they walked in on amateurs night, Nancy hit the stage. She did it as a joke, but the more she danced to the music, the more fun it became. There were four other girls who participated in the competition, and although they received lots of cheers, Nancy took home the crown.

Her performance stuck with her well after that night. She viewed dancing on stage in front of a crowd as a breath of fresh air. Weeks after her performance, she made her way back to the club, this time sober and determined to become a stripper. Once she was hired, she quit school and her internship at a brokerage firm. She took to the stage every night in search of the same limelight and energy it had given her the very first night she stepped foot in front of the crowd. Things looked good the first few months in the business, but slowly the fast-paced life caught up with her and took a toll on her looks. After years of being in the club, her weight had plummeted, and makeup had become her best friend. She'd use it on the regular to cover up her scabby skin and bags beneath her eyes. When you were no longer the new girl in town, the money started to slow, and when the money slowed, additional shifts were taken at a place that ate away at your soul.

Giving herself one last look over, Madison replied to her question. "They want to shake me and throw me off. I can't let them." Madison faced Nancy. "I'll get them back. I just wish I knew how."

Madison's lack of struggling in the club compared to her coworkers made them set out to take her down. Longevity and constant signs of approval weren't seen much in their line of work, so the lack of positivity coming their way made Madison a target. The girls took trying to damage Madison to new heights. Paying customers to rape her, setting the new girls up to steal from her, and sabotaging her sets were some of their futile attempts. Each and every action failed, making their need to take Madison's place as top dancer greater.

Little did they know, Madison didn't have an easy life. She had a miserable one. The misery she encountered tore her down and ripped her apart, the perfect stripper name for a woman willing to flaunt her truth instead of sexuality. Madison's dysfunctional, selfish family transformed her into a depressed soul with low self-esteem and hungry for love. These toxic emotions landed her in strip clubs, which only deepened the dark hole in her heart and nurtured her misery. Although Madison had already felt disconnected from her kinfolk, it came full circle after everyone learned of her stripping ways. Stripping tore her family apart and left her not being spoken to for years. It wasn't until recently that she reconnected with her closest family members.

Growing up, she watched her parents and sister come and go while playing house. It took a toll on her and filled her with resentment and loneliness only the presence of her immediate family could cure. Although she saw them from time to time, she felt disconnected and isolated from them. They were not a family. They were cousins who lived out of town and came in to visit for the holidays. She'd known about her father's other family. Renee was a part that stuck with Madison since childhood. It devoured her self-worth and made her feel looked over twice in one life.

Her coworkers laughed loudly, causing Madison to turn their way and watch them smile nonstop. Right after one of the girls saw Madison looking, a domino effect began, and each girl looked Madison's way. A wave of eye-rolling and snarls followed one behind the other.

"I just wish I knew how," Madison repeated. "I really do."

At one a.m. Madison finished greeting customers she'd catered to throughout the years. She sat at the bar, watching one of the dancers who despised her trying to mimic one of her dance routines. She was so off beat and missed several steps. So Madison just sat back and watched the patrons who knew what she was trying to do ignore the set, which entertained Madison to the max. She and the bartender exchanged hellos before he handed her a glass of water garnished with a lemon slice.

"I've been meaning to ask you, Russell, what made you leave your last job?"

"My boss. His bitch ass would sell his soul for a dollar," Russell spat angrily.

Madison nodded her head while squeezing the lemon into her H2O. "I hear you, but keep your dick to yourself. I know about you burning chicks over there, so don't bring that shit over here."

Embarrassed, Russell looked away and started scratching his upper arm. "Man, I'm good, I got my shot."

"Ummm hmm," Madison hummed. That place was already flying with sexually transmitted diseases, and every day she stepped foot through that door, she made sure to bob and weave. The last thing any of them needed was another disease in there.

The front door opened, and suddenly a number of girls rushed out on the floor from the back rooms. Curious as to what man the girls identified as moneybags, Madison took a look. Quickly, after laying eyes on the man and his goon, she shook her head. Zeke pulled up a barstool next to Madison, and nerves the size of boulders filled the environment.

"What up, Maddy?" Zeke threw his hands in front of him and folded them. He tried not to give away his nervousness, but his bouncing leg took away that option.

"What do you want?" Madison asked, annoyed.

"You didn't come to the house last night."

"I was busy," she replied.

"There's something you need to know. Can you step out for a moment? But first . . ." Zeke looked Madison over. He respected his older cousin more than anyone else in the world, so he asked, "Can you put some clothes on?"

Madison noticed the judgmental expression thrown on her from her cousin and laughed. "No," she replied simply.

Zeke got Russell's attention and ordered a beer. Workers at the club watched from afar, unaware of their gene pool and believing Madison was on the road to big tips. They became infuriated, and their jealousy heightened.

Zeke drank his beer and fought to find the right words. Talking to Madison used to be so easy. Growing up, he looked up to her, and instead of telling people they were cousins, they used to claim they were siblings. She was fun and smart. But all of that changed when depression devoured her, and her dream of becoming a counselor went out the window. Her behavior caused her family to exile her, and Zeke wished he could turn back the hands of time, but they had to abandon her. Watching her spiral out of control was not an option. Finishing his alcoholic drink, Zeke mustered up the courage to tell her what he needed to until he was interrupted.

Stacy, a DJ turned stripper, strolled up to Zeke. She wrapped her arms around his neck and walked in between his legs. "This strip club is not for conversing, Z. How about we go to the back?" Stacy's head tilted to the left, and her high hair bun followed suit.

Zeke roughly removed her arms. The force caused pain to shoot through her arms. His lackey ran to her and hauled her away. Irritation filled the stress lines on Zeke's face due to the large man's slow reaction. Annoyed and now ready for the conversation to transpire, Zeke spoke.

"Madison, Raquel was found in her office yesterday. She was stabbed in the stomach and shot in the head." Finally saying what needed to be said, Zeke waited for Madison's response.

She looked at him, then at all the furniture and people occupying the building. While examining her surroundings, she tapped her fingernails on the bar counter. Seconds later, she slammed both her palms down on the wooden counter and stood up as the last of her sanity withered away and imploded within her. It didn't matter if she felt nothing for her mother. A piece inside of her, a small piece, still believed her relationship with Raquel would have one day made sense. She grabbed the empty glass in front of her and threw it against the bar, her hope for fixing her relationship with her mother shattered.

Chapter 13

From a distance, Madison watched her mother's burial transpire. It was as if time were repeating itself, and the same crippling pain over losing her father slid its existence into the present. Leaning against a tree whose roots had clung to the dirt for many years, Madison dropped a cigarette at its trunk and put it out with the toe of her shoe.

The night Madison found out about Raquel's death, she cried the life out of her body, then fell deeper into the depression she had spent years trying to climb out of. She considered herself foolish for sobbing. Raquel had never been a motherly figure, nurturer, or played any significant role in her life. Yet she was still her mother. Madison remained hidden behind a tree, staring at Carmen.

Carmen never contacted Madison to inform her of their mother's passing. She knew her younger sister made it her business to find out her whereabouts, but she never reached out nor tried mending the gap their parents had built. Unknowingly, Madison continued to bury her shoe into the dirt. Her heart raced and her chest heaved at the sight of her sister.

Carmen stood numb and in complete shock while observing the hole her mother was being placed in. Beside her was Zeke, and behind them, his parents. Carmen was receiving the support and condolences that should have been Madison's. The dark time turned

Madison's stomach and caused dizziness to conquer her vision.

By the looks of her wardrobe, Carmen was well taken care of and without the need of a pole to pay her way. Carmen's tear-streaked face and cracked voice expressed the agony stampeding through her heart. Raquel was actually a decent mother to her, and from a distance, it was obvious. Madison couldn't blame Carmen for following her mother's lead as a child, but as an adult, Carmen was held responsible for her actions. Madison didn't know what it was, why she wasn't wanted or granted entrance into the club she was born into. A large wave of sobs snaked through a line of people, and that was when Madison noticed her stained shoes. Lifting them out of the dirt with her bare hand, she wiped them off and wished she'd never come.

Concealed in the shadows provided by a mausoleum, Dane observed the service given by Carmen and her loved ones. Standing with Julian, Dane had a perfect view of Carmen shedding tears and searching for the strength to keep herself standing. Ever since Renee's exit from their lives, Julian and Dane fed off each other's energy and worked toward Carmen's kill. Seeing Carmen alive and standing in a place where respect was paid to the departed and tears watered the grass over decaying carcasses enraged Julian and drove the need to kill her twice as much.

"Let me fire the first bullet," he declared. "You missed your chance. You staked out her apartment for days and she never surfaced."

"We talked about this," she reminded Julian.

"I know, but all I want is the first shot. You can finish her, but give me the first shot."

Dane and Julian both knew it took only one bullet to end someone's life. One accurate hit puncturing a major artery could rob Dane of her revenge and send her soul lingering in limbo forever. She was lost in Carmen's face. The face that ended relationships, tore apart alliances, and murdered innocent people infuriated Dane just by still being alive. She thought of the accomplishments and success mapped out for her sister, and her heart began to cry. The fairy-tale life meant for Reagan was gone.

"No," she replied.

Emotionless, rebellious, and with every intention of numbing her pain, Dane pulled her gun from its holster and wrapped her finger around the trigger. She walked toward Carmen, firing off several shots. Guests quickly dispersed and separated themselves from the anarchy. Like a sitting duck open to danger, Carmen widened her eyes once she laid eyes on Dane. Fear struck, and her body stiffened, bullets seconds away from entering her chest, when Zeke pushed Carmen out of the way. Zeke's act of heroism left the bullets no choice but to strike Prue, who stood frozen behind Carmen. Prue's body crumpled, the small cannonball stealing her life within minutes.

Falling, Prue's dead weight vibrated the ground Zeke and Carmen lay on. Zeke looked at his mother, her eyes telling him goodbye before he could assist her. Seeing Prue take her last breath caused Zeke's heart to drop and breathing to cease. Staring at his mother's corpse took his soul away.

From a small opening beneath Zeke's body, Carmen lay still and allowed Zeke to act as her human shield. Peeking out from underneath, Carmen saw Dane racing their way. Quickly, she patted Zeke down and relieved him of his gun.

Feeling his Siamese twin separate from him, Zeke looked at his cousin, whose eyes directed him to the madwoman seconds away. Without giving it any more thought, Zeke rolled off Carmen.

Free and able to move without restriction, Carmen aimed the gun up at Dane, who was now positioned in front of her. Both women's fingers went to pull their triggers, but only one manicured nail fired bullets.

Cradling his wife's dead body and shaking while both their hands pressed against the hole in her chest, Roy jumped at the sounds of three gunshots erupting inches from him. Needing his curiosity to be quelled, he saw Dane on her back. Her body was still as Carmen retreated. Roy finally took his sight off the scene when he felt his son pulling at his arm, telling him, "We have to go."

Chapter 14

Working with Jared again brought back a sense of normalcy Renee missed, but she would not admit that out loud. Dane and Metro had plucked out a part of her she spent years developing, and now it was growing back due to the company of a psycho. Her fog-covered mirror was clearing, and she could see herself again climbing to the top without an ounce of rest, fulfilling her zodiac sign as a Capricorn. Life was good, but it wasn't perfect. The cloud in her summer meadow sat in her home on guard and untrusting of her intentions.

Renee's eyes rotated to Calloway, who was mashed deep in a corner of her living room between the patio door and fireplace. For four days, he sat stationed in that nook, stalking Renee's every move. She insisted her ties with Dane were severed and her only motive was to rebuild her life. However, the truth she told sounded fabricated in Calloway's ears. Renee entering the equation broke away pieces of his plan and demolished the security he felt in terminating Carmen and Dane. She had to go. There was nothing Jared could say that could persuade him into believing that Renee was an asset instead of a liability. Having Calloway fill the shoes of his twin brother would benefit him greatly, but if Jared didn't see things his way, he'd kill Jared along with Renee.

"What did she do to you, Calloway? She killed Fergus? She got you back for the secret you hid?" Renee smiled so hard and bright it resembled the lights in the room. She kicked back her vodka trapped within its clear glass walls.

"Jared can't save you." Calloway was so detached from reality and mentally unstable that his mind convinced him the entire world was against him and Dane was one of the reasons for all his enemies. Renee seemed to have picked up the weight Calloway had lost, because his obsession had taken him to the brink of starvation in exchange for sleepless nights in preparation of Dane's and Carmen's executions.

"I don't need him to," Renee growled. Like a magician with the snap of a finger, her smile disappeared, and one of her many alter egos appeared. "Keep it up, and I'ma show you why Dane crowned me queen and left you to clean up my mess."

It was never forgotten that Renee's rank surpassed Calloway's. He cleaned up the messy jobs, which sent him down to the bottom of ditches with some of his victims. Respecting Renee for her savage-like behavior came unknowingly, but questioning Dane's choice of royalty always dangled over his head while laughing in his ear.

Snarling and now at eye level, because Dane had pulled her down by the ankles, Calloway grinned. "You're no longer royalty, Your Highness. You're but a mere peasant, a rodent guarding the palace entrance and getting your hands dirty like the rest of us. You are nothing!" he screamed. The vibration in his voice and volume in his tone raced throughout her home and alerted Jared like a loyal canine to her side.

"What the fuck is going on?" Jared questioned.

Calloway allowed the question to settle before answering, "Just telling Renee that we're all in this together and that there is no more hierarchy."

***

Get to Miami now. Metro.

Repetitively, endlessly, and persistently, Renee read the text and dissected each word typed into the iPhone. She held the phone firmly. Multiple thoughts turned inside her mind as to whether she should take the trip and kiss goodbye the isolation given to her by the couples. Some time ago, the answer would have been simple without giving it a thought, but some time ago had passed and left her mind in disarray.

Why did they want her now? Why were they summoning her when just weeks ago they kicked her out of their club? The comfort she felt with Jared being near confirmed how much she missed the past and how she would give anything to go back to it. But how could she fly back to people who disowned her and deserted her in a time when she had abandoned herself?

In the replica of her Manhattan bedroom, Renee sat at the top of her king-sized bed, analyzing the message. Slow, soft footsteps approached the room on the other side of the door. The termination of movement caught Renee's attention, and her eyes fell on Calloway, who was visible through the slightly ajar door. His judgmental stare locked on the mobile device, then back at Renee. After their millionth stare-down for a total of five seconds, Calloway gradually and sluggishly made his departure.

When first reuniting with the unstable, deranged man, Renee looked to time to cure Calloway's displeasure with her and have it perish into thin air. However, with every day, second, and instant that passed, his distrust in her escalated and seeped from underneath the lid of the boiling pot known as rage. Exercising logic, having Calloway on her side was a highly needed move that would only strengthen her position. However, when his mind was broken and set on retaliation, there was no logic or peace working for her. So focusing on the lengthy and slow footsteps, Renee made up her mind to end their battle of annoyance and unite him with Fergus.

Stepping in her bubble of thoughts, Jared entered her bedroom. His face and aura were less animalistic and more human. His construction boots caught her eye: same style, different pair, walking in a world neither of them had ever stepped foot in and both questioned as to where it would lead them. Taking in her beauty and noticing the silk robe Renee used to wear sticking out of the closet doors caused him to reflect on a time when his love for her was new and unhampered.

He took a seat in a chair decorating the corner of the room and looked at her. A flashback of when she woke up in the dark to Jared sitting in her room crossed her memory.

"If we're going to be together, there are some things I think you should know," Jared told her.

Time slowed, and each person approached the set, acting as the exact person they did the night everything between Renee and Jared went horribly wrong. His need for her love reared its head and spoke as if they were a couple. Working again for Renee was Jared's definition of being together, faith drawing them to one another like magnets.

His belief that they were together withered Renee's selfishness and painted dots of sadness in her soul. She didn't need a body to fall into and lose herself in again. She needed a body to help her win and a mind that she could manipulate and program to do her bidding. Jared expressing his same mind frame from months prior confirmed she had him right where she wanted him, but this time she was not letting him go until her dirty work was done.

"I'm listening."

"The way things ended with us left you in a place I never wanted you to be. I wanted to break you in every way possible, and when I was done, repair you and love you until the end of time. Your lack of commitment sent me to a dark place." Jared stopped speaking, reflecting on the time he took Carmen to bed then agreed to work with her. "I agreed to work with Carmen in exchange for you," he confessed.

The lifeless, blank stare dominating Renee's eyes said more than her mouth ever could. The threats and anger that were spewed the night she told Jared where they stood dug more into him than she could have ever imagined. Believing that they were a couple, Renee could wave it off as puppy love mixed with wishful thinking, but cooperating with the enemy was obsessive. She already assumed he agreed to work for Carmen. Tina had warned Renee that Carmen was looking to recruit for her crew and that she had recommended Jared, but him agreeing to work in exchange for her was frightening.

She was too quiet for his liking. Jared continued speaking. "I wanted you back. You left me no choice. I hope you can understand."

Silent for a few more moments, Renee now understood the love Jared was throwing her way and the person he truly was. "I figured as much," Renee said. "Besides, you were alive, unemployed, and she was in need of a team. What I didn't expect was for me to be the prize."

"Why wouldn't you be?" Jared stood and gravitated beside Renee. "You should be happy I agreed to have you. If not, she would have killed you. The exchange kept you alive. I kept you alive," he enlightened her.

Jared grabbed her chin and forced her to turn his way. Her neck jerked in his direction, her eyes meeting his.

"Are you happy, Renee? Please tell me you're happy." He stared into her face, falling into the ongoing beauty he hoped he would never land from.

The need, the want, the severity in his words boomed throughout her being and gave her plans and ideas of how this man could help her conquer the world. She just had to tread lightly and play the game of conquest as well as him.

"I'm ecstatic." Her lips folded into his, and they sealed their suicidal relationship with a kiss. Jared could not be trusted. He had worked with the enemy for his own personal gain and not for her well-being. That deed could not go unpunished, so like him, she would be selfish.

Brutality and passion filled Jared as he devoured her face with kisses of ecstasy that traveled from her lips down to her belly button. Losing herself in a moment of hunger, Renee clasped her eyes shut. Whisked away in paradise, Jared grabbed her by the sides and laid her higher on the bed. Renee opened her eyes and smiled when she landed on cotton sheets. His shirt separated from his body. He was on top of her. She admired the creases in his chest and bulging muscles. "Breathtaking," she mumbled.

The journey his hands took throughout her body sent lightning bolts surging through every vein and organ within her frame. She forced herself up, with him taking the initiative to strip her of her clothing. She clung to him, her nails penetrating his skin and her lips feeding off his kisses. Pulling from her, he wrapped his left arm around her waist, securing her position. Then, while he stared her in the eyes, his right hand ripped away her sweatpants and panties.

He then flipped her on her stomach, her body crashing on the mattress. She quickly got on all fours. In anticipation of pleasure, she hurled her head back, and Jared grabbed a hold of her hair. Entering her from behind, moans erupted into the air like waves crashing against rocks. He released her mane. Renee's head fell forward, her eyes closed, and her body rocked to the beat of Jared's thrusting.

Cracking her eyes open, she peered at her vibrating phone as a text came through, fighting for her attention.

We need you in Miami. Julian.

Jared pushed himself farther inside, and her mind shifted to her happy ending, interrupted seconds later by her phone vibrating in its seat once more.

I need you. Julian.

As she stared at the phone, her mind raced and took her back in time. There, like a movie, she watched herself as a child lose her father, fall victim to rape, and become verbally and psychologically abused by her mother. She saw her love form and grow for Julian, the young boy willing and determined to save Renee from abuse, the only bright spot in her cloudy life. They were kids transformed into adults who were taken under the wing of an assassin and drug dealer who became family and stood by their side during battles against family and friends.

Renee saw repetitive pain, struggles, and death. She relived ongoing betrayal. Her dire need for family, and ignorance on her behalf, had led her to almost die and innocent hearts of gold to be murdered. Renee's hopes and dreams were front and center, along with shattered love followed by wrecked friendships that sent her down a spiral of grief she'd visited before. It was the same journey responsible for leading her to her current state, where she was consumed by feeling incomplete, desperate, and homesick. These were three components that, when paired with these constant texts, confirmed that regardless of what she'd been through, whatever anger she felt, it didn't outweigh or eliminate the fact that she missed Julian and couldn't go on without him.

Chapter 15

Two Hours Later in Miami

Hours passed, and Madison sat in her car across the street from the cemetery watching the after-events of the shooting unfold. Police officers examined the area and spoke with staff along with mourners. Coroners retrieved Prue's body, and in the middle of it all, Madison watched people try to make sense out of what just happened. It amazed her how no one noticed her. No one noticed her race out of harm's way when the shooting began and then hide out in her vehicle. Even after popping her head out to watch the police scan the area, no one noticed her. So much for safety, since she could have been the murderer hiding in plain sight and no one would have known.

The last three officers at the scene called it a night. Caution tape decorated the burial site yellow and black, as the moonlight bounced off the tape that shook in the wind. *What just happened?* Her eyes witnessed it all, yet her brain couldn't process the events. One second she was angry at the attention given to Carmen, and the next, her aunt was dead. Madison's heart sank deep into her ribs and fought for a comfortable space to dwell in.

Her eyes remained on the area Prue lay in, studying the blood coloring the grass. Slowly they inched to where Carmen had lain, comfortable and protected by Zeke. After Prue was hit, the unknown intruder approached Carmen with her gun pointed directly at her.

This shooting was no mistake. The uninvited strangers wanted Carmen, and they came for her, but instead took Prue. A piece of Madison cheered for the armed woman to shoot her younger sister, but Carmen shot her first. It was clear the instant Carmen saw the opportunity to get away. She took it and left everyone else behind. There was no caring for the family who saved her. Carmen was her only priority.

"Would you die for me?" Renee asked. The sheets clung to Renee's naked body, her sweat acting as glue. Her raccoon eyes grew larger than average and pulled Jared into her world. Lying on his back, Jared didn't speak. Instead, he just eyed her, tracing her features with his vision and falling prisoner to her unnoticeable deceitfulness.

"I'd do more than die for you. I'd leave heaven if it meant joining you in hell," he finally replied.

The comment rocked Renee's soul, convulsed her heart, and severed her feelings. "I need you to come with me to Miami. Metro and Julian need me." She waited for the verbal lashing.

Jared looked forward and fell silent for a moment. "Why?"

"I don't know," she answered honestly.

"Then I'll have to kill Calloway."

The response left Renee puzzled and jumbled.

"If I don't, he'll kill us. Seeing them only confirms the alias he accused you of having the second you sat in his car. You have to pick a side, Renee." Jared looked at her, awaiting her reply.

"I can't without knowing what they want." It pained Renee to acknowledge that her past life was dragging her back in, but at the same time, it gave her relief.

"That solves it. He's dead, and we head to Miami in the morning." Jared sat up. Teetering on the side of the bed, he grabbed his pants from the floor and salvaged his phone from its pocket. Punching his thumbs on the keys, he took the steps needed in booking their flights.

"That's it?" Renee asked.

"What?"

"You're coming with no further questions? We don't even know what we're stepping into."

"Which makes things all the more interesting. Besides, what if they want to make good? I wouldn't want to help Calloway carry out his hit on Dane now that we're together. I don't like her, but I understand that she's your family." Renee instructing Dane to kill Jared disappeared from his mind. Nothing was any longer of interest to Jared. He had Renee, and that's all that mattered.

Renee's eyes dropped. The realization of her and Dane no longer being comrades was disheartening. However, hearing Jared verify why he and Calloway were now in cahoots validated her suspicions.

"And killing Carmen with you would be much more fun than with him." Jared grinned.

Hearing Carmen's name stiffened Renee's blood and tugged at her nervous system.

"Why would he want to . . ." Renee stopped speaking, the curiosity of what Calloway wanted with Carmen fading into a cloud of confusion. The answer didn't matter. Calloway no longer mattered.

"We have a flight for tomorrow morning at nine a.m.," Jared informed her.

Renee nodded her head. He put the phone away, clicked off his lamp, and kissed Renee on her forehead.

"Go to sleep. I'll deal with Calloway. You have nothing to concern yourself with," Jared instructed. He turned his back on her, the sandman's dust quickly putting him to sleep.

Renee stretched her neck, kinks and knots popping with almost every movement. She straightened her back and took a deep breath, her eyes closing and opening. Immediately her sight zeroed in on the bottom of the door. Feet on the other side were visible. She smiled and then turned the lamp on her night table off.

Chapter 16

Sleep was never easily obtained by Renee. Once she fell into a deep slumber, her subconscious would take over, and all that she tried to suppress, eliminate, and devour took over her sleep and relived itself in its true form. For a number of nights, she bowed down to the nightmares and stayed up, watching the hands on the walls clock change positions and the night lighten in color. Renee would lie stiff, whether alone or with company, waiting for time to pass and multiple distractions to occur. That was her typical night almost every night, all except tonight.

She landed out of bed. The cold floorboards broke her feet's fall and chilled their soles. Eerie, loud sounds transpired from the house settling while she walked down the long hall. A gust of wind titled the large picture frames hanging on the walls and swaying in the night, the line of frames guiding Renee to her victim. Under the arch of her living room's entrance, she looked at the back of Calloway's head. Light from the streetlamps shining through the windows landed on his high-back chair. Silence filled the room and was shattered by Calloway's unpredicted voice.

"I'm going to kill you. There is no escaping that," he warned.

"You need to leave the past in the past," Renee advised, her entrance into the room slow and calm.

"I'll leave the past in the past when I put you in it."

Calloway's bloodshot eyes and glossy white skin revealed the toll the loss of his twin took on his soul. His brother's death, paired with the thought of murdering Dane, stole his energy. Calloway didn't want to kill his mentor. She was the only living thing left connecting him to his past life, but out of loyalty to Fergus, he had to.

Now standing behind Calloway, Renee threatened, "You first."

The heavy, oily, dandruff-covered strands covering Calloway's head were enough for Renee to grab and force his head back with. She spat a small box cutter out of her mouth, a hobby she and her baby sister, Page, adapted during childhood, but neither knew they shared. Quickly, she slit a long, thin, and beautifully clean line across Calloway's neck. His body bucked, and his hands shot up to stop the release of blood. Calloway fell backward into Renee's arms, where she slammed the small razor deep into his Adam's apple. Her fingertips lunged inside his flesh, his blood acting as a rosy lotion. Calloway's legs kicked, his vision blurred, and his eyes fluttered, his existence nearing extinction.

"Let the past stay in the past," Renee whispered. She dropped him, his body pounding against the floor. She stood there and took in all of Calloway. She marveled over the darkened bags beneath his eyes and the multiple cracks crisscrossing his lips, identical to the formation of the fresh scars garnishing his arms. The dirt lodged under his nails hadn't gone unnoticed, along with the photograph sticking out of his pocket. She pulled the picture from its safe haven and cleared Calloway's, Fergus's, and Dane's faces of the white residue acting as a mask. Renee's lips struggled to find comfort. They stretched, poked out, and even dropped beneath her teeth. She crumpled the photo, gave one last look at his scars soiled with dried blood, and stuffed the photograph back into his pocket. "Don't ever say I never gave you anything."

She left Calloway alone and dead on her living room floor, only to return shortly with a black case. She dropped herself down beside him, her knees slamming into a puddle of blood. Flying into the air, the red liquid landed on her face. Her hair fell forward. She pushed it out of her face, and blood traveled from her cheeks into her hair. She opened the case, and tools and dismembering necessities shined to perfection sat inside velvet pockets. Renee looked in the direction of her dining room's staircase, hoping Jared remained stuck in bed. This kill was not made for a pack, but the queen of the jungle.

Oversized blackout sunglasses sat high on the bridge of Renee's nose. Miami passed by her window in a sea of blur. Renee sat immobile, yet her mind was an assembly line where numerous thoughts eventually came together and ate away at her calmness. Renee constantly flexed her fingers, her fear of meeting with Dane seeping through.

Beside her, in the vehicle transporting them from the helicopter to their destination, Jared sat calmly. However, he couldn't help wondering what attacked Renee's peace. Her fidgety hands, spaced-out stare, and two-word responses exposed her discomfort. He wished she'd speak to him about how she was feeling, but requesting such a thing was like digging for a needle in a haystack. Renee looked farther into the closed window, her pretend admiration of the town falling short. She opened her fist, and Jared's hand fell into hers. Seeing their fingers intertwine slowed her breathing. Handholding was such a natural, effortless sign of affection. However, it ate at her and built her up all at once. Watching the car swerve into the driveway, Renee squeezed his hand and held her breath.

Chapter 17

There used to be a time when people waited for her and meetings began upon her arrival. Now Renee stood in the small rented beach house waiting for the royalty who had crowned and then dethroned her. Earth tones painted the walls and colored the furniture, and the soothing environment was unsettling to Renee. This place reeked of personalities outside of Dane's and Metro's. That alone worried Renee more as to why she was called. Were there fronts being put up, additional boundaries being made, or was there simply a new taste in interior design?

"I don't know if we're here for a meeting or to meditate," Jared admitted.

Renee tightened her grip on the handles of the square bag she carried around, no longer confident in her gift.

Footsteps murmured from the upper level and made their way down to the first floor. The slow shuffle of feet boomed inside Renee's ears and built a moment of suspense. Renee was sure she heard the floorboards and panels move out of place with every given step. Jared moved alongside Renee, birds in their cages stationed on the living room's end tables, hopping around and chirping. The calm melody was relaxing the two in a moment when they needed to be hard. Only a few feet away, steps were heard turning the corner. Renee could imagine the figures stepping off the last step onto the landing, preparing to make their entrance.

"I see we're moving backward now, huh, Renee?" Metro smirked, disappointment covering his face at the sight of Jared.

"I consider it moving forward, Merritt."

Metro couldn't remember the last time anyone called him by his government name, the name he despised. It took him back to his childhood when that was the only name he answered to. He was forced to bury it when he decided that man couldn't take him where he needed to be. The rage erupting from Metro's chest was evident through his breathing pattern. His chest couldn't deflate, and his breathing wouldn't quiet down. He moved in closer to Renee, his quick movements forcing Jared to step in front of her, king protecting queen. From behind Jared's shoulder, Renee smiled. There would be no repeat of what transpired the last time they met. Metro locked eyes with her and stepped back, the imagery of him hitting her too vivid and overpowering to avoid.

"Thank you for coming," Metro told Renee, showing the aggression he once held at bay.

Now that Metro was a comfortable distance away from Renee, Jared removed himself from between them.

"What do you want?" she spat, the question burning on contact.

"Dane needs you, so come with me." Metro disappeared the way he entered.

Swallowing, Renee closed her eyes and took a deep breath. There were but so many emotions she could hide, but so many walls she could continue building. Shaking her head to rid herself of her discomfort and the resentment she felt toward her mentors, she pushed herself to get answers.

On the verge of separating herself from Jared, Renee told him, "I'll be right back." With her free hand, she touched his face, and then she quickly instructed her feet out of the room.

Around the corner, she bumped into a waiting Metro. "Welcome back."

Renee's left hand grabbed ahold of the banister, her right hand gripping the handles of her bag so tightly it hurt. Tired of the tit for tat, she threw caution to the wind and tossed the bag at Metro's feet. She hadn't imagined revealing its contents this way, but timing no longer mattered.

Eventually, Metro dropped on one knee and unzipped the bag, backing up fiercely into a wall. The stench it held threw him backward and jumbled his thoughts. With a scrunched-up face, he looked Renee's way. Her unresponsive stare pulled him to the bag again, and this time he looked inside. What lay within the carrier occupied his attention for quite some time. He had to tear himself away from the visual.

"My peace offering," Renee expressed. "I fucked up. I know that now, and it will not happen again."

"Is that Calloway?" Metro questioned. Pulling open the bag more, he observed the decomposing head staring back at him.

"Yes, and next time it will be Carmen. Consider him the appetizer." Renee's response was cold and inhuman. She kicked the bag to the side, and Calloway's head rolled out.

Closing the space that divided them, Metro raced over to Renee and pulled her into a hug. "This is what I was waiting for. This is how you should be at all times. Whenever family is harmed, you fight. You never tap out," he instructed. Not all love was the same, not all love made sense, and not all love was kind. In some families, normal families, ties are cut once you hurt, let alone try to murder one another. However, in highly dysfunctional, unstable, criminal lives, love is determined and gained through loyalty and is proven based on the pain cast on the enemy.

Renee closed her eyes, tears drizzling down her cheeks. Things were the hardest they'd ever been between her and the power couple. Each took dangerous and disrespectful steps against one another, but when it was all said and done, the comradery and love couldn't conclude. They lived in a world where pain connected them, the type of pain many hadn't and would never experience, so she couldn't hold a grudge. She wouldn't hold a grudge.

After seconds of feeling their circle slowly reconnect, Metro broke the silence. "Make things right with Julian, and whatever you built on your own bring into the business. Let's start over."

Renee's eyes shot open. The thought of Julian stiffened her body and stole her comfort. Julian was a different story. He did what no one could. He captured her heart, built it up. He made her feel, made her love, and dared to seek a pain-free life. Julian made her human only to crush her.

Immediately, Metro noticed her shift of happiness. He pulled away. Focusing on Renee, he noticed Jared peeking around the corner. "If you can forgive us, you can forgive him, so make it right not for us, but for you." Metro looked at Jared once more.

Before responding, Renee, for once, listened to what her heart had to tell her. She allowed it to speak without silencing it and downplaying its emotions. Renee paid close attention to the reactions it gave her, the good, the bad, and the indifferent. She weighed which stood strong and which dissolved not long after being given a thought. Drying her cheeks, Renee nodded. "Which way is your room?" she inquired.

"The second door to the left."

Renee jogged up the steps, preparing herself for her meeting with Dane. Dane and Metro's bedroom door was shut. Before entering, Renee listened for a sign of movement, a tip as to what she should expect before entering. Renee didn't know why she couldn't open the door. She had made good with Metro, the one who voted her off the island, yet she couldn't face Dane. Maybe it was because part of her resented Dane for not standing up for her and allowing their friendship to be thrown away.

Before she punked out and lost the strength to open the door, Renee turned the doorknob and walked inside. Sunlight crashed inside the room from the terrace's slightly ajar doors. The smell of lavender sugar drops floated in the air, and bamboo furniture shined against the light. The bedroom's tropical aura was a medicine many dreamed of bottling and selling but never could capture. Renee ran a hand over a fluffy pillow positioned on a chair with the stitching of a kitten on it.

"It's all too calming, but Metro thinks I need to relax. He thinks tranquility will help clear my mind and strengthen me. But little does he know the anger festering inside of me is what makes me want to get out of this bed," Dane said.

On a massive bed surrounded by pillows, Dane sat up, her body drowning in cotton bedding. Renee's heart collapsed when she zeroed in on the bandage applied to Dane's head and the cuts and bruises on her arms. She marched over and flung the gigantic pillows plastered with images of rainfalls and exotic flowers off the bed and plopped down.

"What happened to you?"

Dane smirked, her head seeping into one of the oversized pillows. "Would you believe that little bitch got me? The first time in years a bullet knocked me off my feet."

Storm clouds darkened Renee's eyes and sharpened her rage. "Carmen."

Dane's lip curled. "She knocked me off my feet, but not off the earth. The bullet grazed my head, and two others hit me in the chest, but Lucky over there took one for the team." The battered bulletproof vest she referred to as Lucky sat snug on the glazed wooden chair.

It took a lot for Renee not to stampede through Miami in search of Carmen and put down the monster she should have gotten rid of a long time ago. It was always on her agenda to delete Carmen when she discovered the truth, but being stripped of all her connections set her back. So she took some time to rebuild, revamp, and reorganize her life in order to give Carmen the pain she deserved. But her shooting Dane took things too far and confirmed she had to take her out and quickly.

"Maybe it wasn't such a good idea for me to crash her mother's funeral." Laughter trickled out of Dane's mouth. The thought of Carmen's pain was all that kept her sane while she was forced on bed rest by her husband. No real damage was done to Dane, but Metro feared her mind would step out on her. The mind was a powerful thing, but when undergoing several traumatic events, it could weaken and give out if not cared for. So Metro ordered Dane to rest and sink into a state of peace. However, no matter how many days she rested and listened to soothing music, Dane continued planning her next move. Metro putting her in time-out did nothing to help heal Dane. All it did was help her strategize.

For a while, neither spoke. It was something that needed to be done before they hashed out the past.

Without looking at Dane, Renee proceeded to say, "I'm—"

"Don't you dare," Dane cut in. Her face was hard and still. "We're even now."

It was hard to ignore, forgive, and accept what Dane and Metro had done, but it had to be done. After examining the situation, Renee now understood their point of view and knew it was time for things to go back to normal.

They were now even. She failed to take immediate action against Carmen, and they repaid her by dethroning her. There was nothing else they could do to harm one another more than they already had. They'd played their most vicious cards.

Renee looked at Dane. "This has to end."

"And it will," Dane responded.

The fidgeting and sweating of Renee's hands left her palms dry and brittle. She walked to the dresser and grabbed the lotion closest to her reach. Smudging a fair amount into the center of her hand, she moisturized her hardened skin and picked up her head to see Julian standing in the terrace's doorway. The sight of him threw her back to when she watched him on her terrace playing a game of chess the day she arrived back home from Jamaica. They made love then, a home reunion she ached for and sank her all into when finally receiving it.

The lotion slid on her hands, her body heat melting it off. She fell into his gaze with the undeniable need for a connection roping around her heart and tugging her forward. Dane repositioning herself stole Renee's attention. Dane's weak appearance caused Renee to snap together the realization that if Julian was still associated with Dane, then there was a possibility he was at the shooting too. Renee snapped her neck Julian's way, instantly looking him over for wounds.

"I'm not hurt," he answered. The ability Julian had to read Renee's mind was still strong and accurate.

"Only me and a family member of Carmen's were hit. It ended almost as soon as it started," Dane informed her.

Renee's lips balled up, her sight resting on the floor. She wanted to feel Julian's flesh in order to guarantee that he was okay. She wanted her lips to meet his and tell him, "I'm glad you're okay," then connect on a physical, mental, and spiritual level. Losing her breath over the thought of reconnecting with Julian, Renee took a deep breath and made her way to the door, the intensity all too much. Yet before walking out, she told Dane what she was sure she'd be happy to hear.

"I brought a gift for you and Metro, Dane. Tell Metro to give it to you." Renee then left her body leaning against the door and let out her breath before making her way down the stairs.

"What do you think she has for you?" Julian asked, his eyesight fixated on the door.

"According to the size of the bag she brought in on the front door's security cam, body parts. Fingers, eyes, and toes, hell, maybe even a head."

"They were in a blind spot where they had their conversation. Did you listen to her conversation with Metro on the intercom?"

"Yes, and if I'm correct, whatever is in that bag belongs to Calloway, I heard them say."

"She brought him with her," Julian interrupted. He didn't really care to talk about what was in the bag. He only entertained the conversation until he no longer could. Concrete images of Renee entering the house with Jared haunted him. He wished he had never watched the security cameras.

"He's here for security purposes only. You of us all should know how she moves," Dane reminded Julian. She sat herself up more, laid her head back, and prepared for a nap. "He'll be gone just like Calloway. Once she lets you back in."

Chapter 18

It didn't seem as cold. It didn't seem as nail-biting, toe-numbing, or circulation-stopping.

This day just seemed . . . average. The sun melted a majority of the snow, sending it down the city's drainage system. Carmen rubbed her arms, the only thing soothing enough to keep her mind at ease and on guard at all times. Her touch kept her on high alert, a reminder that what was taking place was real and not a dream she wished upon a star on many nights for it to be.

Her hair missed her brush, and the dark blotches underneath her eyes missed her concealer. The corners of her mouth were cracking, and dead skin threatened to fall with the mere movement of her mouth. She was breaking down, her wafer-thin fingers in great need of nutrition. In the back of her mind, she knew that being queen was a task that came with many detrimental outcomes and traumatizing experiences. Yet she thought she could avoid them all. She thought she could keep her hands clean by dirtying the hands of her pawns. She underestimated it all, thinking she was smarter and more conniving. But in Carmen's case, she learned the hard way.

Every now and then, Carmen looked back at the house whose steps she sat on, trying to avoid looking at her aunt's house across the street. For two hours she sat on that step speechless as to what she would say when she entered that home, *if* she entered that home.

After the shooting, Carmen became hysterical. Like a nomad, she wandered from place to place, never feeling content enough to rest her head at one spot for long. On day three of her searching for a new place to find refuge, she decided to head to New York. She'd do better among her family and would less likely be harmed because of a barrier known as her cousin.

The house she sat in front of was nice, her choice of style. And she was grateful the owners weren't home to shoo her off their property. The sun began to set. When the temperature decreased, Carmen stood up from her seat. Grabbing her luggage, she struggled to carry the heavy suitcases across the street to her family's estate.

Standing in front of the door, Carmen dropped her luggage beside her feet, conjured up the saddest expression she could muster, and waited for her cue. At first, she knocked softly, then harder when she heard nothing and no one answered. Her fist banged against the mahogany door until it opened and her fist fell inside. Having gotten an answer, Carmen kept her eyes to the ground and away from whoever stood in the doorframe. She needed to seem believable from the beginning and wanted whoever was watching her to see she was remorseful. Her breathing increased, and her eyes watered. It was a scene from a soap opera spat off a television screen. The family's mourning had no room to feel for Carmen, but she needed them to, and she needed their sympathy. It was insurance for her survival.

Tears skied down the slopes of her cheekbones. She rubbed her shoulder, and when her performance didn't receive a response, she looked up. Her mouth dropped and became dirt dry. Her crocodile tears were a failure. There was no pulling the wool over these eyes.

The woman walked outside, her long-sleeved shirt the only barrier between her and the winter's night. Her sweatpants were baggy and full of movement as the door closed behind her. Carmen backed up, her heart beating like music pulsing through headphones. She searched the woman's facial expression, hoping she could read her mind. Minutes passed, and the woman said nothing, not a word, just taking in the vision of her little sister. Then finally, after years of Carmen not hearing her voice, she said, "Those legs you used to run away while Aunt Prue lay dying in her own blood led you here. What business do you have with us?" Madison was calm when speaking.

Carmen was astonished that the first thing her older sister said to her in years dealt with an incident that had taken place only days before. It was heart stabbing, an unbelievable reality check that her family died with her mother.

My mother, slid through Carmen's mind. She never properly mourned the older version of herself. Carmen cried some, hit and broke a few things, but never did she taken the time to actually feel.

"What do you want?" Madison rudely asked, her voice heightened as she stepped a bit closer to her sister, intimidation lingering in her movement.

"What's wrong with you? Aren't you happy to see me?" Carmen stupidly asked.

Madison chuckled. "Happy to see you? Where the fuck have you been? You search for me but never reach out, and when I'm not throwing a parade because you show up at *my* family's house, you want to get emotional. I'm going to ask you one more time, what is it that you want?"

Shock drifted away, and anger at how she was being treated after hours of finally collecting enough strength to knock on this door forced Carmen to spit out, "What do you want from me? You want me to apologize for being the one our parents kept around, or do you want me to apologize for not running to the strip club to witness my sister shaking her ass? I'm the youngest, the baby. Maybe you should have reached out to me, " she spewed.

The surge of anger that traveled through Carmen's chest was a feeling never felt before. There were multiple feelings parading throughout her, determined to escape. The blow was low, swift, and breath-stealing. Carmen had enough of the ongoing disrespect during a time when she needed someone to console her, hug her, and tell her everything would be okay. However, she was crawling to people who were damn near strangers, in search of protection because she dug herself a grave a number of people were trying to push her into.

As she stepped closer, Madison's shirt blew in the wind and slammed against Carmen's coat. She towered over Carmen, literally big sister and little sister. She caused her sibling to step backward and off the property.

"Your mother really led you to believe you're special, her baby, her Mini-Me." Madison's fingers combed through the strands of Carmen's hair that fell from its clip. Madison remembered Raquel telling her to brush her hair a hundred times a night, and she did, alone with her mother's voice guiding her in her head. Carmen's hair was soft, a product of a hundred strokes per night and a validation that their mother taught the one thing she shared with Madison to her sister. There was nothing for only Raquel and Madison to share, no bond.

"I don't know what you want, but whatever it is, you're not getting it here," Madison told her, her voice filled with emotion. "You've had everything, so whatever need you have that drove you here will not be fulfilled, I can assure you of that." Madison had no idea about Carmen's dealings, but she would block anything and everyone from helping her. Carmen's brat train ended here, and Madison's daggers for words made her a new enemy.

The look on Madison's face was a work of art, a replica of how Renee looked when she too was angry: the curve of the lip, plunge of an eyebrow, and tightened of a cheek.

"You can't do this, Madison. You don't know what you're doing," Carmen stressed. Without Zeke's help, she was dead, a third member of their family dying within a span of a few weeks.

"I know exactly what I'm doing. I'm stopping the person responsible for Prue's death from hurting this family further. You did nothing during or after the fact. Those people wanted no one but you, and after Zeke saved your life, you ran, leaving them all to fend for themselves."

Real tears flooded down Carmen's face. "I had to," she babbled. "They would have killed me, and they'll succeed if you don't let me inside. Please let me make things right," Carmen begged.

Madison's head jogged up and down. "So that's what this is about? You're scared, and you're looking to Zeke for help." Getting the answer she really wanted, Madison bypassed Carmen's vulnerable moment and set her eyes on the house behind her. Every time she visited Prue's home, she looked at that house, a habit she formed for no true reason. Seconds later, Madison continued speaking to Carmen, her connection to the house dwindling.

"You're cancerous, like your mother. Whatever you touch evaporates. I heard about Lyfe and Benz. I know more than you think. They dealt with you and magically died, just like that. I bet you had something to do with it, and I'll tell you what, you will not bring that strand of bad luck over here." Turning her back on her sister, Madison jogged up the stairs leading to her aunt's, disappearing behind the door, then slamming it shut.

Carmen ran up to the door, her balled fist in the air, determined to put a dent in the wood until she was granted access, but she couldn't do it. She couldn't enter her family's life after meeting with Madison. She was irate, her body shook, and she stormed off, kicking trashcans on her way down the street and leaving her luggage where it sat.

Zeke watched from behind the living room blinds as she disappeared down the street, the malicious words never secretly shared between the sisters.

Chapter 19

Renee timed it. Every five minutes, the ocean crept to shore and wet the sand. Her steps were large, but every time her giant steps landed in the sand, she was met with the waves saturating the gravel. The cold water relieved her hot skin. "I have an older sister," Renee whispered. She didn't look Dane's way, only farther out into the beach. She didn't know what sat at the end. She knew only that it was ongoing.

"A letter was left behind when we went back," Dane admitted.

Renee nodded. She tried to digest everything Dane had told her about the murders, the letter, and Julian.

"I can find her," Dane suggested. She tried reading Renee's thoughts and imagining how she felt when visualizing meeting another member of her family she knew nothing about. A member she could possibly look up to and pray was normal.

In two minutes, the waves would cover Renee's feet, so she waited for the salt water, hoping its coolness would help center her thoughts. Quicker than she thought, the cold liquid slammed against her feet.

"She's not my sister. She's Carmen's. There is not enough room for both of us in her life. This is bigger than a sibling rivalry. We want each other's heads. Given the choice, if you were this new sister, who would you choose?" Renee's head snapped in the direction of Dane.

Dane thought it over, and Reagan came into view, then a stranger whose facial traits held their own, and her decision was made. "But what if she's different, an outcast like yourself?"

"What if she's one of them? A self-absorbed savage?" Renee challenged. After a moment of silence, a question clicked inside Renee's mind. "Why do you care? Why are you trying to form a relationship with Carmen's sister and me?"

"Because I worry for you," Dane admitted. "Because I know that I will not be here forever, and when I'm gone, you will have no one. It will comfort me to know you have at least one person."

"I have Julian," Renee answered. The comment rushed out of her mouth and stiffened her legs. Renee didn't intentionally develop the sentence in her mind. It was created in her subconscious and flew out of her mouth.

Dane slowed her pace and gave Renee enough room to gather herself and speak her truth.

After taking a deep breath, Renee let it all out. "I just can't forget, can't get the imagery of them together out of my head. But every time I see him, for the first few seconds, I forget it all and instruct my feet to race into his arms. But every time the first step is taken, reality hits me and I remember. I picture her with him and smell her on him, and that's when I lose it, lose everything we have ever had." Tears slid down Renee's cheeks, the memory of love freshly engraved in her heart and soul. "I miss him, but at the same time, I need him away. I just don't know for how long."

In front of Renee, the beach seemed longer than it had minutes prior. Accepting that she was walking toward nothing, she stopped and plopped down on the hot sand.

"How do you forgive and forget?"

Dane stood for a moment. She searched in the sea for an answer to give her protégé. "There's no one answer to that question, Renee. Different answers are meant for different people. You just have to dictate which is yours. You can leave, sure, you already have, but is this where you want to be? Is your heart meant to be separate from his? Is this the best decision, or what you *think* is the best decision?" She paused. "Or you can go back, but if you do, track down your relationship's dismantled pieces and fix it. Dissect what went wrong and operate on it, learn from it, and never turn back. Become one instead of living as two."

While speaking, Dane never looked at Renee. She was lost in the movement of the sea and in the words of her speech. Her legs wanted to sit but wouldn't. This wasn't the time for comfort, but a time for peace.

"Did Metro ever cheat?" Renee asked.

Dane shook her head. "No."

"If he did, would you ever take him back?"

Without delay, Dane responded, "Yes."

The severe honesty and quick response caused Renee to gasp. She was sure Dane's response would be grue-some, cold, and unforgiving. However, the opposite was given, and it made Renee think over her and Julian's situation more. "Why?" Renee wanted to know.

Dane wanted to give a long-winded, heartfelt, fairy-tale-ending response, but she couldn't. Her mind would not conjure up one, because the only answer she had to give was, "Because I love him." Sometimes life worked in ways the human mouth could not explain and the mind could not comprehend, or even create to express. So Dane spoke from her heart.

"I still love him, Dane," Renee revealed. For so long, she hid from those feelings. And now that she was vulnerable, she had to admit it, had to finally free herself of emotions. "And I want to go back."

Dane sat down. Renee's face was full of tears. "Then go, but let Jared go."

Renee's heart dropped. Jared was a creature not meant for her, a creature who was attracted to her pain, darkness, and isolation. He gave her what she needed when she couldn't deal with what was meant for her. And the blow she was about to give him, she questioned if he could handle a second time around.

"He won't let me go."

"He won't want to, but he'll have to," Dane answered.

"What are we going to do with Carmen's cousin? Before she's dead, I want to strip her of every connection she possibly has and tear down her life just like she's done mine," Renee expressed.

Dane knew Calloway would find his way to Zeke. Her number one rule was to research her prey, and that was exactly what Calloway did. Calloway knew Carmen's cousin would eventually cross paths with Dane, but before she did, he wanted to have killed Carmen, taking away the one thing Dane lived to do. So Dane connected with Zeke in order to stay one step ahead.

Dane understood where Renee's question came from. Now that Zeke had proven to protect his family, it was time to cut all ties immediately, and Dane knew just how.

"How quickly are you willing to let Jared go?"

The question was weird, off-topic, and head-scratching. Renee looked at the ocean, the tide coming farther onto the shore. It touched her skin, and the comfort reminded her of Julian. A smile stretched across her face.

"Like yesterday," she replied.

"Then use Jared for one more thing, and throw him away like he never existed."

Chapter 20

"Why didn't you tell us you were at Raquel's funeral?"

Madison was seconds from the kitchen until Zeke's voice pulled her back. "What are you talking about?"

"Raquel's funeral. Why didn't you tell me you were there?"

Madison rewound to her reuniting with Carmen yesterday and wondered what Zeke knew. "What does it matter?" she asked.

"You know the truth. You saw it all. Carmen may be too dumb to ask questions, but I know better. Why didn't you say anything?"

"Why didn't you tell me this shit is all because of Carmen?" Madison challenged.

A question answered with a question. Madison's query trumped Zeke's, because the least of their problems was whether she was on the guestlist for her mother's funeral. The issues they adopted from Carmen were priority and now endangered them all.

"I didn't think you needed to know. Dealing with two deaths is enough. There's no need for me to anger you more."

Madison sat on the satin, cushioned chair seated next to the living room's entrance.

"I'll take care of it," Zeke assured.

His cousin's eyes squinted, and her face cramped together. "Take care of what?"

"The people after Carmen. The people responsible for destroying your mother's funeral and killing mine."

Madison's eyes moved in every direction possible, and a crooked, uncomfortable smile settled on her face. "You're going to take on her problems, the reason for all of this sudden mayhem?" she had to ask before jumping to conclusions. Madison had to make sure he was saying what she thought he was and not speaking in a foreign language.

"What else would I do? Did you not see what they did?"

"Yes! I saw my selfish brat of a sister bring death to our front door, and now you want to help her? Do you even know these people who are after her?" Madison saw no need to run to the defense of a person who could not sincerely apologize for their wrongdoings or check in on their family's well-being.

"Fuck what Carmen has to do with this. That bitch killed my mother!" Zeke's breath increased, and his blood pressure turned his skin pale and hot. Dane killing his mother was chiseled in his memory, and he blamed himself for working with the enemy. Now he saw that, for whatever reason, Dane had used him and maybe Carmen too. He should have cut all business ties with Carmen the moment he decided to, but he couldn't think about that now. He had to think about killing Dane.

"That bitch was aiming at Carmen. It's because of your dumb ass that she missed." Madison's words were hurtful but, at the same time, correct. Zeke was thinking more with his emotions, while Madison thought with her head. Was what happened right? No, but Madison believed nothing better would transpire from joining a war they had no part in from the beginning.

Zeke stood from the couch. His mouth was glued shut, and his emotions were on a rampage. The comment Madison made repeated itself in his mind. "You don't need to remind me of that, but still that woman's reasonable. I know what I'm up against. It won't be easy, but it won't scare me away either. You should have let her in, Madison."

And just like that, history had repeated itself. Another family member had chosen Carmen over her, and the feeling of abandonment started to ease in. Anything except the truth was acceptable, and now Madison witnessed it with her own two eyes. Zeke tried to make an exit. However, Madison's loud speech slowed him down, his feet dragging on the brown carpet he'd taken his mother to purchase.

"She's a stranger, Zeke. Family or not, we know nothing about her. Don't do this. She never even called to see how any of you were doing after the shooting. She ran and left you and Uncle Roy like sitting ducks after you saved her, and she damn sure was not here to take responsibility for what she caused. She's a user. Don't fall for it," Madison begged.

"And what the fuck did you do?" Zeke lashed out. "What the fuck did you do to save us? Where were you, hiding somewhere? Why can we take you back in and not her? What makes you so damn special?"

"Not a motherfuckin' thing," Roy interrupted. Roy stepped inside the living room he'd given his wife full range to decorate. His entrance was slow and full of negative energy, his tight face harboring pain in need of a release. "You have issues, little girl, if you think we are going to stand and let my wife's murderer go free. If my son wants revenge, no one is going to stand in his way." Roy loomed over Madison.

"You're thinking with your hearts," Madison told them, "and not with your heads."

"You damn right," Roy shot back. "And if you can't respect that, then respect our home and get the fuck out!"

Madison's family kept throwing her away. They kept pushing her off the moment she did things they didn't agree with, and now that it was happening again, she didn't think she could forgive and rebuild. Madison nodded her head. There was nothing she could say for them to see things her way. To suggest they leave Prue's killer untouched was craziness, and when she said it to herself, she understood their disagreement. However, Madison was looking deeper into the error of their ways. She was examining Carmen and predicting that if they kept her under their wing, more travesties would follow, and no one would ever be happy.

Roy walked away, and Zeke stood broken by the days' past events. He knew what streamed through Madison's thoughts, and he comprehended that, after she left their home, they would never see her again, because once again they had exiled her. "There's still time to see things our way," Zeke pleaded, his last chance of keeping Madison inside of the family.

"And there's still time to see things my way," Madison insisted. She knew that it would never happen, but they still had time to take back what they said before she cleared out the room she'd had there since she was a child. The same room was left untouched when their family bond first broke. When Zeke didn't respond, Madison got up and left the room, hours of packing ahead of her.

Zeke sat on the chair his mother always rested in. And for the first time since her passing, he took a deep breath and examined his life. His leg shook, a simple, quiet way of releasing his grief. Cool air entered the room and dried the emotions appearing on his cheeks in the form of liquid.

With a few taps on his phone's screen, he searched for new text messages. From the corner of his eye, he noticed the deserted luggage he'd retrieved from outside tucked behind the living room's curtains.

He expected to hear back from Calloway, but instead, Jared responded. The new additions to his crew would be the perfect people to handle his dirty work. He'd use whom he was paid to keep an eye on. They had to be a threat for Dane to be watching them. Satisfied with what Jared wrote, Zeke jumped out of his seat, grabbed the luggage, and rushed out.

Chapter 21

This was no television show where, after Madison finished packing, she would stand in the middle of her room and reflect on all the good times, and a pinch of fear, regret, and sadness would suddenly wash over her and make her fight to stay. No, this was the straw that broke the camel's back and the last time her family would push her away.

Two suitcases and three duffle bags were scattered around the room, the empty shelves, dressers, and closets giving off an echo. Madison wanted out. Refusing to sit one last time on that bed, she stood and dialed a cab. Immediately, she heard the busy tone, which led her to roll her eyes and dial once more. On a Saturday night, this was no coincidence. All lines were busy. The sad thing about it was that this was the only cab service installed in her phone, and going out on icy sidewalks to hail a cab with five heavy bags was not in her future. And still, with all this taken into consideration, Madison refused to use Uber or any other of those new car services, Madison was old school and left those upgrades to the millennials.

After she called for the fourth time and received the same response, Madison's cell phone chirped with tropical birds singing to the rise of the sun, informing Madison of an incoming text. It was Nancy, and if Madison wanted to be specific, it was Nancy texting for the tenth time. They all read the same:

Where are you? Are you trying to get fired? These girls are over here having a ball talking shit. Just let me know your dumb ass is still alive.

Madison exited the text and dialed the cab service once more. She had disappeared from the job without informing them that she'd be attending her mother's funeral and never bothered reaching out when she landed back in New York. After everything she'd encountered, she didn't think she ever would.

Beep. Beep. Beep.

Pressing the end button so hard she nearly broke the tip of her finger, Madison flung the chair from underneath the vanity table and crashed down on it. The drawer slid out due to the rumbling, and a pack of cigarettes showed itself. Madison's goal was to throw her bad habits out the window, but if she didn't find a silver lining somewhere in this dark cloud, she'd find herself somewhere jammed in a straitjacket. She lit a cigarette and, for a few minutes, released aggravation out into the lung-slaughtering smoke. With her free hand, she used the tip of her long, colorful nails to write Nancy. The nicotine awarded her the clarity she needed to form a sentence.

I'm okay, and tell them bitches to keep my name out their damn mouths!

Her mentioning her coworkers shouldn't have even made it into the text, but when it rained, it poured.

Where the fuck have you been? I went to your house every day for the past week and you weren't there! Nancy wrote back swiftly, her timing confirming that she was either off work or finished with one of her sets.

I'm not home, Madison wrote back.

Since you're all secretive and shit, can I use your shower? I'll sneak in that shit if I have to. This funk I'm carrying around is becoming unbearable.

Madison put her cigarette out in the ashtray paired with the Newports. Her chuckles aired out the poison she'd inhaled. She forgot how good it felt to laugh. Positivity held on to her and allowed time to slip away. Throwing the cigarettes into her purse, she made one more call out to the cab service. Her change in demeanor must have blocked the negativity, because the line rang, and after answering destination questions, the dispatcher informed her that her vehicle would be there within three minutes.

Madison's cell phone chirped. She rammed the phone inside the pocket of her jeans, slipped into her coat, and grabbed the two suitcases. Like a penguin, she wobbled from side to side, speed walking so that she could relieve herself of the heaviness at the front door. Dropping the suitcases on the doormat, she rubbed her arms and then jogged back up the steps for the rest of her belongings. When everything was situated at the exit, she opened the door and came face-to-face with a younger version of herself.

The cab honked its horn while Madison stood planted to the ground, examining the stranger's bone structure and stature. The cab driver rolled down his window and screamed out, "You call a cab? You coming?"

Madison dropped her bags, her stare never shifting. Instead, she threw her hand up, signaling for him to leave. Madison stepped back. Not only was their physical resemblance uncanny, but also the aura Renee gave off. Renee was her: a sister she knew about but had never met, a sister who, if their family were different, she could have possibly bonded with.

"How are you?" Madison asked. After seeing so many pictures of Renee as a child while snooping through her father's wallet, Madison always wondered how she'd look as an adult, and now that question was answered. "It's nice to finally meet you." Madison extended her hand.

Renee's forehead caved in. "Who are you?" Renee became uncomfortable, her guard increasing instantly.

"I'm Madison, your sister," Madison told her, her hand still held out.

So this is she, Renee thought. Without notice, her body fell tense.

Renee hadn't prepared herself for this. She had no plan when it came to meeting Madison. In fact, she didn't know that she ever would. Renee imagined herself giving her condolences to Roy and moving on. However, looking at this mirror image of herself, she wondered if subconsciously she knew Madison would be there and if that was the real reason she even cared to come by.

The stay at Dane's Miami home had been a short one. Renee's visit seemed to brighten Dane's behavior and get her off bed rest sooner than Metro had anticipated. Landing in New York two hours ago, the team followed Zeke back to New York, confident he would bury his mother where she lived and create a distance from the Miami turmoil. Leaving the airport, the five adults parted ways, but not before Jared and Renee partook in a kiss that sent Julian's insides spewing with violent anger.

Julian marched away, refusing to watch the "couple" engage in an emotional goodbye when he suddenly stopped. He needed to look back once more to make sure his relationship with Renee was truly over. The kiss was still taking place, but when Jared pulled away and jumped in a cab, Renee caught Julian's eye. She wiped Jared's kiss away, batted her eyes, and wrapped her arms around her waist. For the first time since she found out about Julian's infidelity, she actually looked like she loved him again. Julian walked her way. People walked back and forth in between them, blocking his view of her, then allowing him to see her and vice versa. When he was seconds from reaching Renee, Dane grabbed him and led him in the opposite direction.

"Not now. In due time," she whispered.

Julian didn't know what that meant. He looked over at Metro, who nodded his head, confirming the truth in his wife's words. Renee went home alone that night with no worries concerning Jared being out on a job. She walked in her home and, after looking out her window, felt compelled to give her condolences to the family she'd grown to know.

Ignoring the formalities and Madison's introduction of herself, Renee told her, "I'm sorry about Prue. I live across the street and thought I'd give my condolences." Renee pointed backward at her home.

Madison laughed, her hand dropping and slapping against her leg. She wished Renee at least shook her hand, but she understood the disconnect. She let out a heavy sigh. Today was a bad day, and it only seemed to get worse.

"Prue mentioned the new, pretty neighbor who reminded her of me. And if it means anything, she didn't know who you were. Never even knew how you looked." Madison's eyes zeroed in on Renee's home. *At least I know why I couldn't keep my eyes off this house.* "Thank you. I appreciate you coming by, and I'm sorry for your loss as well. I know how fast you two became friends."

Discomfort continued to invade Renee's body. This was the most awkward moment to date. She didn't know what to do or how to act. Should she just walk away, leaving behind yet another family member and ignoring once again what she wanted—family? Or was she to jump into another tank infested with fish called "sisters" who turned out to be sharks?

"Let me know when the funeral is. I'll think about attending." Renee didn't know what she thought she'd get out of possibly attending the funeral, but she brought it up anyway. Turning around, she looked back at her home, which appeared to be miles away. She wanted to run away from the drama known as her family and disappear. Speaking with Madison further could result in too many issues. Too many things had been done, would be done, and she could never turn a blind eye to Carmen's wrongdoings. Renee could not forget that she was the odd sister out, but for some reason, she couldn't walk away.

"You want answers, don't you?"

Renee heard Madison speaking, but she didn't acknowledge her and didn't pull her gaze away from her home.

"You want to know things. I understand. It's natural, but you will never ask because you think I'm like Carmen." Madison chuckled some more. *No matter what I do, Carmen will always haunt me.*

Renee faced her. "She is your sister."

"Was my sister," Madison corrected her.

Renee gave her her back and walked away. Madison reached out and grabbed her arm. Renee looked at Madison's hand wrapped around her upper arm. *What is with the women in this family, grabbing people?* Renee asked herself.

Madison looked Renee straight in the eye. "I'm not Carmen."

"Let me go," Renee warned.

"Listen, I have a lot of issues concerning Carmen, but none of them has nothing to do with us being alike. I have been abandoned by this family more than once. I will not have another back turned on me today." Madison's hand never separated from Renee's arm. She didn't know where this strength came from. Maybe it was from being pushed over the edge more than once.

Renee snatched her arm away. "You're not like Carmen, because she's not crazy enough to touch me."

"I'm sorry, but you really shouldn't judge what you know nothing about. Let's talk. Let me get to know you."

"You don't want to know me," Renee responded, her boots smashing leftover snow beneath her feet as she walked across the small street.

"I know I want to fill in the blanks for you about our father!"

Renee's Achilles heel, her kryptonite, or however you wanted to describe her father, stopped her in the middle of the street. She thought Lyfe had filled in all the blanks regarding her father, but then again, before she knew who Lyfe was, she never knew there were blanks to be filled. Renee's hesitation was enough for Madison to react. She dove back into the house, bringing the rest of her belongings out, and slammed the door behind her. The tropical birds started to sing, a reminder that Madison had an unchecked text message.

Holding on to a few bags, Madison walked over to Renee while struggling not to fall on the ice. Her head pointed toward the house. "Shall we?"

Renee's face wrinkled. "I shall, and you shall not," Renee informed her.

Madison dropped her bags. "Our father threw his two other kids the leftovers of his time because you and his wife were his priority. I'm coming in," she insisted.

"I never knew about you or Carmen until recently, especially you. And the person responsible for killing Prue and your mother is my mentor. Since meeting Carmen, she gave me hell. Now her life is on the clock, and I will kill her. Now, do you still want to get to know me?"

And there they were, the facts that would separate sisters before they came together.

"Fine." Madison smiled and jammed her bags into Renee's hands. "Now, tell me about your childhood."

She retrieved the rest of her belongings from in front of Prue's house and headed over to Renee's, unfazed by her honesty and determined to get out of the cold.

As Madison stood in front of Renee's doorstep, waiting to be let in, Renee continued to stand in the middle of the street oblivious to what was taking place. Renee looked down at the luggage and back up at Madison.

"I'm no longer welcome there!" Madison screamed. "And why travel home at this time of night when there's a sister of mine who lives right across the street for me to learn all about?"

Chapter 22

Jared sat in the hotel's lounging area, staring at the entrance. His lack of movement and silence created an uncomfortable feeling in each of the hotel workers' stomachs, which led them to constantly watch him.

"He's been sitting there for an hour. What do you think he's waiting for?" one of the clerks questioned her coworker.

"I don't know," the short girl with neatly twisted locks responded, "but he's creeping me out. He's not talking, moving, or nothing. He's just . . . there."

Jared noticed the looks being given to him, those fearful glances in the eyes of many. People wore their emotions on their sleeves and never bothered hiding them within themselves, so to stumble upon a person they could not read hindered their comfort zone and made them become suspicious of the unknown. Individuals from all walks of life came and went from the temporary place of residency. However, none were the prey Jared was ordered to demolish. An hour early to his agreed appointment, he took heed of his surroundings, dissecting the place chosen by Zeke to meet.

This kill he would cherish and carry out with precision, simply because it would be the first he'd accomplish while officially being in a relationship with the love of his life. There were no more disruptions between the two or a time of absence keeping them apart. It was just Renee and Jared, and to celebrate, he would give her what she asked—kill Zeke. Zeke was in the wrong place at the wrong time and saved the wrong life. Even though this story could be turned in so many different directions, it landed in the direction where they must rid themselves of future problems and allies who could eventually help Carmen.

Jared was lost in a world where only he and Renee existed and time stood still. His eyes remained cemented on the rug. A faint gush of wind carried Jared out of his thoughts and pointed him in the direction of Zeke, who walked quickly past him toward the elevators with luggage in hand. The fast steps awarded Jared the idea that he would drop his belongings off, meet with him, then stay the night, another customer in need of service.

After pushing the button for the elevator, Zeke stepped inside and the doors closed. Moments later, Jared took his place in front of the elevators. He watched as the numbers lit up and finally froze on the number four. Aware of where the establishment's staircase was, Jared took to the steps. Jared made it to the fourth floor just in time to see Zeke headed in the opposite direction, his focus straight ahead.

Jared's boots sank inside the soft navy blue carpet, its material taking away any indication that a savage was near, on the prowl, and determined to slaughter its victim. The distance between the two gave Zeke the advantage to reach his room safely. He withdrew his room key, slid it in the slot, and let himself in.

Zeke being out of sight did nothing to increase Jared's speed nor worry him. At a normal pace, he continued to walk down the brightly lit hallway with freshly applied wallpaper. Along the way, he inhaled the flowers propped up in vases that were plucked early that morning. Women covered in penis necklaces and other bachelorette party accessories staggered out of their rooms while talking loudly to one another as if they were miles away instead of shoulder to shoulder. When pink sashes and crowns turned the corner and were out of view, Jared stood in front of the door Zeke had entered. He knocked. Its lurid yet harmless banging masked the danger that stood on the other side. Stillness filled the room, and Zeke glanced at the other breathing body looking his way. "Room service," he mouthed.

Zeke pushed away the peephole's metal covering and listened to it click-clack. Many hotels withdrew from having peephole covers, but not this one. This roadhouse was against Zeke and worked in Jared's favor 100 percent. It was the reason Zeke didn't see Jared first, the reason the carpet masked footsteps and the numbers on room doors jumped around, making it challenging for him to find room 404 within seconds. Zeke lowered his head, looked through the peephole, and before his vision cleared and straightened to perfection, the peephole exploded. A bullet entered his eye and traveled out the back of his skull.

The sound of a large thump and the quietness that followed hummed throughout the hall and turned Jared around, leading him downstairs to the hotel's lobby. The lobby appeared more crowded than before, including the presence of security, which was entering the building just as Jared fled the scene.

The uniformed man reentered his post he had abandoned for a half hour. His partner was out ill, so the responsibility fell all on him, and it was the perfect time to earn some money without having to share it. He sat in his seat and turned the cameras operating throughout the hotel back on. His excuse for the delay was unthought of, but the $5,000 he made would help him come up with something.

***

Blood and membrane slid down the walls, seeped inside the crevices of the floors, and ruined the couch's cushions. Dry air swarmed the room from out the open window, and the hole in the door caused the air to circulate and shoved the stench of blood and feces inside Carmen's nostrils. Waste released from Zeke's bowels after his death.

Slowly Carmen breathed in and out, her limbs never moving from where she stood the moment Zeke hit the floor and his life ended. His blood looked finger painted on her face and arms and sprayed on her clothing. She didn't scream, not once. Not even an hour after his death did she utter a word or think one thought. Instead, she remained in shock, her eyes blinking at a calm rate.

Carmen had separated herself from the pain she felt in her cramped neck while frozen. Pain swept along the side of her neck when she finally moved it. Reality was disclosing itself. The lost world she ran to was drifting away and appearing further and further away the more she fought for it. She saw directly through the hole the bullet had left behind, the room across the hall in clear view.

No one has come. No one had peeked from behind doors or peepholes to answer to curiosity. An hour had passed, and no police invaded her room and questioned the event. *He had a silencer,* Carmen finally noticed. She looked around and didn't stop until she saw the luggage her cousin was returning to her. It was ruined, dark blood spots on its leather. She was cursed. Anyone who hung around Carmen for more than a day was tugged inside her fight and removed before they could fight back.

She told her legs to move. However, the signals she was sending did not reach their destination. So she tried once more. Her feet moving in small steps felt like she was walking for the first time. A tingly sensation associated with falling asleep took over. Carmen fought against it and walked over to the luggage. She collapsed, landing on her knees, pain radiating through her body and forcing her silent. Her mouth agape, tears eased from her tear ducts. And like rain, more followed and created a rainstorm. It was not going to end. Nothing would end unless she surrendered, and that was something she couldn't do. She knew that submission meant she agreed to dying and losing a battle that she started. Although she couldn't throw up the white flag, she also could not continue like this.

Her cousin's body commanded her sight, and she wondered what he wanted to speak with her about. Earlier, he called her to say he'd return her things, and when he did, they needed to speak. They agreed to meet at her hotel, the same hotel he told Jared to meet him at. His plan was to speak with Carmen regarding erasing Dane, and then go downstairs, where his meeting with Jared would take place. There they'd make out a blueprint as to how they would carry out his revenge.

Zeke's cell phone was halfway out of his pocket. Carmen took it and swallowed the urge to throw up. A slather of blood sat on the front of the phone. She rubbed off as much as she could on a clean article of her cousin's clothing. She needed to make sure whoever was responsible for this was who she had in mind. Zeke had enemies outside of her own. First, she searched through his call log, then his text messages. That's when she saw the conversations Zeke held with Dane and Calloway and, lastly, Jared. He worked with them, and, with what she could tie together, things went wrong because, the day he saved her, they discovered they were family.

The phone slid out of her hand, and Carmen's head tumbled forward. She couldn't do this anymore. Her last attempt at help now lay beside her. Her protection was gone. She grabbed the coat closet doorknob and pulled herself up. She walked inside the bathroom and rummaged inside her makeup bag. A variety of pills sat next to her eye shadow, mascara, and lipsticks. Some were meant for sleeping, depression, and the pain Carmen's body had been under due to the stress she had experienced throughout the last few weeks. Medication was a need and never far from her side.

She popped the cap off three bottles and littered them on the bathroom sink. They mixed and matched, and the glass of water she'd never finished the night before stood tall. She scooped up a handful of pills and stuffed them in her mouth. These pills once temporarily helped her, but now she needed them to work permanently. Emptying her warm, stale glass of water, she sat on the bathroom tile floor. With her back and head against the wall, arms hugging her knees pushed against her chest, she waited for death.

Chapter 23

Astonished, grateful, proud, nervous, intrigued, scared, and confused were all the emotions pooled into one ball of feelings welling inside of Renee. Renee and Madison spoke for the remainder of the night, and still, the conversation carried on as each woman threw out past and current life events. The two went back and forth sharing experiences, some of which were presented for the world to see and some that were locked in boxes buried beneath the earth. This was a time of growth.

Madison managed to get Renee to speak openly and without regret. Renee's change of emotions showed on her face. The happy, sad, angry, and nonchalant reactions showed with every story she told. The connection was odd. A stranger she had just met hours ago seemed to be turning into her best friend and peeling away years of hardened layers all in one sitting. How their lives mirrored one another's led to a direct understanding on both ends. Both women were in need of family, and although they were in the same city, they'd never crossed paths until this day. Renee's relationship with Page and Carmen held no weight in comparison to the communication she and her older sister were now developing.

Listening to Madison express herself and even give advice showed Renee that she never knew how to be a big sister. Her playing the role never worked. Renee's life went incomplete for years because of lessons she never learned from Madison. Now that Madison was here, she wondered, had the four sisters been in each other's lives from the beginning, would life as a family have been happier?

Renee was not the only one who had learned Madison was nothing like Carmen. Hearing Renee speak and watching her listen to what came out of her mouth showed Madison that she was by far a different species from Carmen. Renee took an interest in what Madison had to say, and when it was her time to speak, she spoke honestly. Madison received no indication that Renee was self-absorbed or a menace to their family. She was just like her: wounded in the line of fire known as their bloodline and seeking to heal the best way she knew how by pushing through.

Madison didn't want to admit it—in fact, she probably never would—but being disowned a second time around would have made her an orphan. The pain of that fact would have torn away at her insides and caused life to wither away. Renee appearing at Prue's home was a godsend. Their one-man-band of a family had just become two.

Mexican takeout containers, wine glasses, and a diverse collection of snacks covered the living room table. After a while, tiredness was winning as the women fought to stay awake. In order not to conk out, they sat silent for a minute. Renee's head lay back on the fluffy couch pillow, and Madison's eyes closed and then opened when she felt herself going under. After thirty seconds of falling asleep, Madison's eyes popped open and landed on the Christmas tree.

"You do know it's March, right?"

Renee looked at her, drowsiness fogging her brain. Madison nodded toward the tree, and when she saw Renee looking in the tree's direction, she laughed at her months of neglecting to take it down. A half-smile made its way on Renee's face when she looked back at her sister.

"Oh shit. I'm one of those people who keeps decorations up for so long that by the time they take them down, the holiday is right around the corner again." The two laughed, Renee's discovery of a new characteristic entertaining and embarrassing. She sat up. Looking at the tree again gave her words to say. "I guess you can say I became a different person when I moved here."

Madison closed one of her eyes while keeping the other open. "What are you talking about?"

"When I lived in Manhattan, all of my decorations went up and came down in a fair amount of time. Things were never one hundred percent happy for me, but at times life was at least bearable, and then new problems came up. When I learned about Julian, I just shut down and checked out. I had nothing left in me and, on countless occasions, contemplated suicide. I been through some shit, but that was just soul-shattering." Renee leaned over, resting her folded hands on her knees.

Madison opened both eyes. Renee's words acted as coffee and woke her up. To hear her say it was "soul-shattering" stole her attention. Growing up, she always believed that when something was broken, it was repairable. Like if a vase fell and broke in two pieces, it was possible to mend it. But if it was shattered, there was no going back. The pieces were too small.

"And then the anger kicked in, an anger I never felt before, when Dane and Metro ostracized me. Everything hitting me at once, knocking me down, and not giving me the chance to breathe and get back up made me feel like shit. I always considered myself broken, but having all that fuckery happen at once made me feel like nothing. I was dead inside, and the only thing that kept me alive was the anger and revenge." Renee looked at Madison. "That scares the shit out of me." Tears welled in Renee's eyes. "To have such negativity be the reason you're functioning. What does that say about me?"

Renee was no angel, but after years of pain and growing numb to any emotion, she decided to retire. It was after that decision had been made that she finally felt alive again, tasted happiness, and wanted no part of a world she spent most of her life in. This was, of course, months before finding out about Julian's infidelity. So when bad times entered and she fell deeper into depression, it scared her to have recently experienced happiness. Instead of latching on to that to get through the hard times, she fell back into old habits.

Madison removed herself from her position on the loveseat and joined Renee on the larger couch. "It says that you were hurting. It says that you reverted to the negativity simply because you didn't want to feel the pain. And instead of going through it, you chose to go around it. It also says that because you acknowledge how you acted, you will never do it again." Madison's sentence flew out of her mouth like a speech written and practiced days prior. It came out effortlessly and from a genuine place. It came out so effortlessly because it was something she told herself every day and wished someone had told her. Madison always wished for someone to be there for her and make sense out of the confusion, but now that she sat with Renee and took notice of her troubles, she no longer wanted to be helped. She wanted to be the one who helped.

Renee wiped her tears away. "Is that how you felt all those years? Angry and living off pain during a life you knew was not meant for you?"

Shock waves shot through Madison's veins, and uneasiness ran in. She never mentioned feeling as if her life as a stripper was not meant for her. She never offered an opinion on the occupation at all. She only stated facts and voiced why she was there. Yet hearing Renee conclude from her life story that it was not meant for her, a hard life or not, was a reality check that she really didn't belong where she put herself. Madison being a stripper was an exact example of trying to force a square into a circle.

"Yes," Madison answered. "That's exactly how I felt, just a walking host of anger, looking for anything to help me ignore it, but the only problem is that it's back." Madison tried to force a smile, a failed attempt at concealing what she felt was not as bad as it really was. The drowning feelings of abandonment were back, and although Renee cut off the bulk of the pain, it was still there, and Madison feared its return.

"Do you want it to leave?" Renee asked.

Madison smiled. "What kind of question is that?"

"Then stop stripping."

Madison shook her head. "You're judging me now too? You haven't known me for a total of twenty-four hours, and you too have something to say?"

"You said you want that feeling to leave. You claim you want to put it to rest, yet you're still doing what you ran to to help you escape. Now, if it helped you in any way, let me know now, and I'll never speak on your occupation again." Renee waited, waited for a positive to stripping she knew would never come, and it didn't.

"I can't leave right away," Madison admitted. "I have to do what I have to do until I can get myself together. Money does not grow on trees. Trust me, I know, because every day I look out my window hoping."

Renee giggled. Laughter truly was good for the soul. "Don't worry about that. Your sister got you." They used the word "sister" from time to time when referring to one another, and because it was used prematurely in their relationship, it struck them both stiff whenever their ears heard the word.

"I'ma have to get used to that. Renee . . . my sister." Madison's words trailed off while she tried to get used to the sentence. Birds chirping interrupted their conversation.

"What is that? I heard it all night but waved it off, thinking the wine had me tripping. Now I know it's not that," Renee said.

Madison stood and retrieved her phone from the pocket of her coat hanging on the coat rack. "It's a text. Every time I heard it, I said I was gonna check it and never did." Madison's phone lit up for her to see a total of ten text messages waiting for a reply and several missed calls. The first few were Nancy telling Madison to hurry back because the club's dancers were being reckless with their mouths. That was three hours ago.

These bitches done lost their motherfuckin' minds. All our shit we left here is gone. We have nothing. No vanity table, costumes, or customers. They wiped our asses out. We're motherfuckin' blacklisted. I don't know how they did this.

Madison, fuck this place! I know a good three spots that would love to have us in their joints. Fuckin' Stacy got our asses and got our asses good. I don't know what the fuck happened when I was off, but no one wants anything to do with us, not even our boss. Ain't that some shit? You saved his business, and he's throwing your ass out in the cold. By the way, he told me to tell you since your stank ass don't wanna work, stay the fuck out.

Fuck this! I ain't going out like this. I'ma tear this motherfucker out before I leave. I'ma be like that dude from Breaking Bad. They're going to remember my name.

Madison, call, write. Fuck, send a motherfuckin' smoke signal. I'm heading home now. Fuckin' Kirkman threw my ass out, but not before I tore up the DJ booth. That pussy-ass motherfucker, why did I give him the na-na in the first place?

The texts stopped, and the time stamp showed they resumed a half-hour later.

We're blacklisted, Madison, and I'm talking about all over. We can't get work even if we worked for free. Damn! I'm screwed.

The remainder of the texts consisted only of Nancy telling Madison to write back and freaking out about being out of work. Nancy had words with the girls, but the small spats did nothing to take matters this far. She found her way into Madison's problems because she was her friend, and a friend of Madison's was an enemy of Stacy's. Deciding whether to leave that lifestyle literally came at the perfect time. However, it bothered Madison that her friend lost employment because of her loyalty. Madison told herself one day she would get them back and, now that they got her and her friend fired, she'd handle things. Ignoring and playing things cool could no longer happen. She exited the texts, smirked, and placed her fingers on her chin, repressing her anger and maintaining her sanity.

"How much weight do you really carry?" Madison asked Renee. It was happening, the anger she and Renee just talked about, the need for revenge festering and attempting to fall out by any means necessary.

"What?"

"You're the queen, right? Is it really true, or just a myth?"

Renee didn't know where this conversation was heading, but Madison's tone and questions sat uncomfortably and disrespectfully with Renee.

"Do you want to find out?" This came out as more of a threat than a question. Madison was new in Renee's life, but no matter how much they clicked, Renee would never make the same mistake she made with Carmen. *One strike and you're out,* Renee thought.

Madison smiled and flopped down beside Renee. "Yes. Why don't you show me?"

***

A key inched inside the lock, quiet and with ease. This key had never been used or approved. Its existence was not known. But it was here now, and its use was mandatory. A light click echoed throughout the house, warning carefully listening ears that an uninvited guest was present. However, the warning was missed, along with the creaks the floors gave off. Slacks falling over the back of shoes brushed the panels, and a shine glowing in the morning sun pulsated through the living room blinds. Footsteps stopped, and someone observed his surroundings, strolling from room to room on the first floor. Making his way back to the foot of the stairwell, he saw duffle bags and locked luggage snuggled against the first step. A piece of denim peeking through a small, unzipped portion of a duffle bag informed the intruder it had recently been tampered with.

The cushioned stairs took the form of the size tens. No squeaks were made against the house's foundation. Instead, it contained the noise and kept up the morning peace. Reaching the second floor, sounds of water drowned the ears of the invader. Rooms fell behind the intruder, his head peeking inside the opened doors and ignoring the closed ones. This uninvited guest followed the sound of dripping bathwater. His pace slowed just a little but increased when the shower water spilled out louder. The golden doorknob granted access to the royal quarters.

His hand reached for the bathroom's doorknob, yet one second before touching it, it pulled away. The need to admire her skin, feel the water, and take a voyage throughout her body pushed him forward. He received flashbacks that screamed like a cat in heat, but still, he resisted. Step by step, this gentleman walked backward and didn't stop until the bed stopped his movements. He sat down, eyes fixated on the mahogany door.

Renee plunged her face into the hot shower water. Drops of H20 banged against the back of her neck. She had not slept, had yet to fall victim to her pillow and sink into a world of relaxation for hours of reenergizing. After five more minutes in her personal spa, she stepped out, her feet landing on the plush navy blue bath rug. It absorbed the clear liquid escaping from her body. Water splattered on the zigzag-patterned titles when she stepped off the rug, and it created a slippery surface. She dried herself off and threw her towel back on the towel rack. When it fell, she stuffed it inside the slim opening, the thick towel bulging out. She opened the door and stepped inside the bedroom with her head down.

Heading for the dresser, she looked up and looked directly at Julian, the winter's cold from the open window tapping Renee on her naked body.

"How did you get in here? Did Madison let you in?" Her arms folded against her chest, but just enough to act as a push-up bra and heighten her cleavage.

"Does it matter?"

It didn't, and Renee didn't push the issue, because deep down inside, she really didn't care.

Her tight body stood firm, exactly how Julian remembered. He analyzed her curves and saw where she had lost weight. He knew the depression he caused her had contributed to that. Julian looked back up into her eyes. "Who's Madison?"

"My sister."

Silence. He believed Dane when she said she told Renee about Madison, but it was better to hear it from Renee himself. When quietness swallowed them both whole, Renee turned toward the dresser. She opened the top drawer in search of nothing in particular, just a reason to keep herself busy. She fell into a world of undergarments when a pair of hands touched her skin.

She jumped, her eyes landing on Julian's reflection in the mirror. The discussion that took place between their eyes and lips could not translate or duplicate their emotions. She finally turned around and laid her head down on his shoulder. Renee closed her eyes and lived in the moment. She had fantasized about this moment, pieced it together, and devoured the feelings. Following the reunion images she had set up in her mind, he turned her face toward his, their lips bumping into one another's and making her fantasy a reality. The soft, gentle kiss intensified, and they kissed into each other's souls. Tears dampened her cheeks, adding to the emotions locked within their surroundings.

"I'm sorry," he whispered, the apology leaking out of the corners of their mouths.

"I know, and I love you." She pulled from the kiss and gazed undividedly into his eyes. The sins of their past vanished. "I love you more." Julian hoisted her in the air. Her legs secured themselves around his waist as they took off to the bathroom.

Steam raided the bathroom and fogged the mirrors. Water splashed out of the tub, Renee and Julian didn't bother to close the shower curtain and drenched the floor. Slapped against the blue-tiled wall, Renee welcomed Julian back into her temple and released liquids of her own. Water splashed over the sides of the tub and spilled on to the floor. It avoided Julian's clothes, curving around the material and floor mat, and rushed toward the entrance, where it crashed into Jared's Timberland boots.

Chapter 24

"He made you take the pills?" Officer Reynolds asked, his left hand scribbling in his notepad the details being mentioned to him by Carmen. It saddened him that every time their paths crossed, it was in reference to some type of pain she was in. Their first encounter ensued months ago when he and his partner delivered her the news pertaining to her uncle's death. For weeks, he couldn't get out of his head the scream she let out. He heard it while sleeping, investigating crimes, and whenever he was rewarded with a time of silence.

"Yes, that is correct," Carmen answered.

It was three in the morning when she and Zeke were finally found. One of the young girls attending her friend's bachelorette party saw the hole inside Carmen's room door and, with caution, took a look. The alcohol in her system rumbled and shook her stomach while vomit inched itself upward. But for confirmation that there were no wounded people in need of help, she swallowed the chicken wings, nachos, and French fries she partook in hours prior. Carefully, she entered the room and found Carmen sitting unconscious and spilled over. The sight of Carmen's blood-ruined clothes forced the vomit to escape her mouth and squirt all over the bathroom. It took a moment for her to get herself together, but the release of liquids and food actually helped sober her some and give her a clearer state of mind. Dialing 911, she stayed with Carmen in the bathroom, fighting off the smell of stale blood and puke. She kept telling herself that she either dealt with that or the sight of a man with most of his cranium missing.

Travel time to the nearest hospital took minutes. Carmen's stomach was pumped, and when everything was said and done, she fell into a deep slumber. Her mind and body were in dire need of rest. Carmen recalled dreaming about a cat racing past her and jumping pebbles, bushes, logs, ditches, and boulders.

She followed its fast movements to the point where she made herself dizzy and her neck cramped. However, her curiosity was at an all-time high and could not rest. The hurdles the cat jumped seemed to get more dangerous than the one prior. It started off light, then grew to leaping over oceans. Each was a success and a mind-blowing sight to behold.

Carmen lost count of the hurdles the cat jumped. Was it the eighth, ninth, or tenth? The fire-raging pit seemed to fall deep within the earth, a relative of Dante's inferno. The cat stopped, her fast feet kicking up dust while coming to a pause. And then it looked at her. Inside, Carmen cheered her on and was excited to see this trick emerge. But the cat didn't run, didn't amaze or amuse. Instead, she just stared, then without warning disappeared. Carmen looked around, took steps around the grass-filled field, and stopped when the cat appeared in front of her face.

"You have nine lives," the cat told her. "Nine lives." Then she disappeared.

That's when Carmen woke up. It was the best sleep she ever received. Unfortunately, sleep did not come easy these past few weeks, so after the gastric suction, her fears and stress were no more. Her body demanded that she rest. It had no energy left to fight the battle she signed herself up for. And although her dream was mind-boggling, it made her proud. She was a survivor who jumped over many hurdles. It made her see things in a different light.

When she took those pills, she was tired of fighting, tired of running and every time being found. Carmen checked out mentally for the moment, and that friendly cat brought her back. She was now reenergized and approached with the strength needed to fight Renee. Her mind was now clear, fresh, and sharp as the first day she stepped foot in New York, and she was going to use it to manipulate the police. Not long after she woke, the detectives came in and questioned her about her cousin's death and her overdosing.

"Why would he force you to overdose and not kill you like your cousin? He's killed before, so why not do it again?" Detective Day questioned.

"I don't know," Carmen whispered, her throat sore from her stomach being pumped. "I don't know why. People do weird things. Maybe he wanted it to look like I killed my cousin then tried to kill myself. Maybe he didn't know we were cousins and took us as lovers." Carmen was laying it on thick, taking herself out of the situation she knew well and pretending to be an outsider looking in. She wiped the tears plunging from her eyes and let that act be the icing on the cake. The cherry on top was when she looked their way and revealed, "I know him. I know who did this."

Reynolds flipped a page on his notepad and ignored his partner glaring at the side of his face. *This may be the easiest case we've taken on in a long time,* Reynolds thought.

"Who, Ms. Hunt? Tell us who did this to you."

"His name is Jared, Jared Psyche. He's not wrapped too tight. He's hurt me before, but I never thought it would go this far." She cried, and this time it was ongoing, a nonstop attempt to win them over with her bullshit story. "We were together at one point, nothing serious, just a fling here, a fling there," she lied. She stretched her one-time sexual experience with Jared into several.

"If you guys were not serious, why would he do this to you, and what had he done before?" asked Reynolds.

Carmen paused and swallowed. "The first time he laid hands on me, it was because I went to his house unannounced and found his home empty and him leaving. I'll be honest with you. I was angry. He told me nothing about a move, so I demanded answers and asked him what was going on. We argued. He didn't like me questioning him, and before I knew it, he was choking me." More tears dropped, and Carmen quickly started to wipe them away. "I'm sorry," her hoarse voice let out.

"Why now? Why come and do all of this? Why not kill you when he had the chance?" Day asked.

"Be easy," Reynolds interjected. "She's the victim here."

Day gave his partner a look, an agitated glare that screamed, "Let me do my job."

"Why now, Ms. Hunt? What happened after he moved, and is there any other reason you think he would go so far as to kill your cousin?"

Internally, Carmen was smiling. The cops were now on two different pages, and all that was left for her to do was flip Day over onto her and Reynolds' page. She turned away and focused on the window and the family members entering and exiting the hospital. Today was such a beauty. Winter was slowly leaving and making way for the next season.

Day called out to Carmen, "Ms. Hunt."

"I threatened him," she spat out. She took a deep breath, pretending that she was preparing herself for the bomb she was about to drop. "My cousin was a drug dealer, Jared is a drug dealer, and the two have done business together. I knew about this because he didn't know Zeke and I were family and that he told me everything. After what Jared did to me,"—Carmen paused, clearing her throat and momentarily giving her voice box a break—"I wanted to get him back and make him just as afraid as he made me when I thought I was going to die that night in his house. So days later, I contacted him and told him that if he didn't give me ten thousand dollars, I was going to the police with everything I had on him pertaining to him selling. That really pissed him off, but I didn't hear from him for a long time after that and never received any money. I really didn't want it. I just wanted to fuck with him, and I did, so since I heard nothing from him, I let it go. But trust me, if he had given me the money, I would have taken it." She smirked.

"When Zeke came out to New York and reached out to visit me, that's when this all happened. I don't know how Jared knew exactly where I was. And I can only assume that him seeing Zeke there that night was a wrench thrown in his plan."

Reynolds nodded. "One more thing, Ms. Hunt, and then we'll be out of your hair." He placed his hand on top of hers. "How does Jared look, and where does he live?"

Carmen gave the officers a rundown of Jared's physical features, from his towering height down to his distinct tattoos. "I don't know where he lives now. He never told me," Carmen stated.

"Thank you for your cooperation, Ms. Hunt. We'll be in touch." Reynolds gently caressed her hand, a smile landing against Carmen's face.

The detectives left the room, and Carmen sat proud of her performance. She rolled over, got comfortable, and prepared for a quick nap. Soon she would undergo a psychiatric evaluation. She'd need every trick filling her bag to pull this one off.

"You're a real piece of work, Reynolds. A real piece of fuckin' work," Day voiced. He was never one to fall weak over a pretty face, so to see his partner all googly-eyed over a pill popper boiled his blood.

"Should I have accused her of attempting suicide and murder like you?" Reynolds spat.

"The shit makes no sense. Why not kill her? If she was the reason for going to the hotel in the first place, why not kill her also?"

"Like she said, people do weird things, and you should know better than anyone else that weirder shit in this world has happened."

"So now you're abandoning your cop instincts and going by the word of a broad you want to fuck? Good job. I gotta tell the captain to give you a promotion," Day spat.

Day thought back to his wife and why he took a vow to do his job and do his job right, which required him to wear no blinders. He wanted to make the world a safer place for his better half to exist in. However, if he was going to do that, he had to toughen up and carry an umbrella at all times, because he never knew when a shit storm would hit. Day slammed his palm against the elevator call button.

"Let go of the bad-cop routine, and put that old memory of yours to use," Reynolds instructed. They walked inside the elevator, and Day didn't respond until it closed.

"What are you talking about?"

"Jared Psyche is the little fucker he's been hunting for years. The son of a bitch Lane wanted to put away just before he retired."

Day thought for a moment. "The girlfriend killer? You talking about the kid Lane had on his radar when he was on the force down South?" Things were starting to click inside Day's brain. "Are we talking about the same fucker who when he came to New York bodies would pop up, yet he always slid through the cracks?"

"Exactly," Reynolds confirmed, scratching his neck. "The same guy Lane was after, but there was never enough evidence to convict him with."

The elevator doors opened, and both men stepped out, their thoughts fresh and now sharper.

"I couldn't give a damn whether Miss America up there is telling the truth or not. I just want Jared's ass. We can use this to put him away. So I say we question the staff and visitors once more in that hotel and see what we can scrape up. Someone has to know something. I'm not buying the whole 'our cameras weren't working for a few hours' bit by that security guard," Reynolds stated.

"What about her cousin? She said he was a drug dealer."

Reynolds opened the car door. "Consider him a casualty of war, one less scumbag we don't have to deal with. I want the bigwig, so let me know when you're on board." Reynolds got into the car.

Day smiled and hopped in, proud of how quickly his partner bounced back and came to his senses. "I'm down," Day ensured.

"Good." Reynolds pulled away from the hospital and merged into traffic. Minutes later, he broke the silence. "Be real. She is fine as hell, though," he commented, a large smile plastered across his face.

Day just shook his head, his moment of being proud of his partner gone.

Chapter 25

The bathroom door connected to Renee's bedroom was wide open. The bathwater led a trail of H_2O from the bathroom and stopped at the foot of Renee's bed. The water glistened, adding to the serenity brought to the home that morning. She slept in bed that afternoon. The sun shined bright through the window and hugged Renee's face. She turned her head, her legs and arms intertwined with Julian's. The two melted together, yet Renee still snuggled closer. Burying her face in Julian's chest, she started to moan, annoyed with the sunrays disturbing her sleep. Without opening his eyes, Julian squeezed her tighter. The security she felt wrapped in his arms instantly brought her comfort. The bedroom door cracked open, and then there was the loud noise of Madison's scream as she quickly tried to close it again.

"Madison," Renee called out. She turned her head toward the door.

"I'm sorry. I didn't know you had company," Madison apologized.

Covered in blankets and sheets, no skin was visible. However, the cracked door brought a little more air inside than Renee cared to have, so she buried herself farther under the blankets, her body sliding down Julian's. Renee continued to snuggle beneath the covers, strands of hair the only proof she was there.

"That's Madison?" Julian asked.

Renee felt the vibrations in Julian's chest when he spoke. She pushed the covers down a little from her face. "Yeah."

"Was that her luggage downstairs?"

"Yes. She only stayed the night. Last night her uncle kicked her out of his house since she didn't agree with them wanting revenge. It was late, so instead of traveling home, she came here."

"How did you meet her?"

Renee came out from underneath the covers, a gush of air filling her lungs. "I went to give my condolences, and she opened the door. Would you think I was crazy if I told you we talked all night about everything?"

Julian stood quiet, listening to Renee.

"I told her everything, Julian."

"Does she know who you are?"

"Yes. I stopped hiding when we all separated. Anyone I come in contact with knows who I am."

Julian said nothing, and Renee felt his chest slowly rise then fall. She sensed his discomfort over her exposing her identity. Doing so placed her in harm's way, but that was what you did when hurt.

"She knows about the hit on Carmen and Zeke. She even knows we're responsible for her mother's death."

Julian opened his eyes and looked down at the top of Renee's head. "And she's fine with that? How can anyone in their right mind be willing to stay at the person's home whose associates killed their family?"

"I don't know, but she is."

Silence fell over Julian. To relive the same events they went through, but with a different sister, was sure to break them all. He wished he and Renee could slide under those covers together and have them act as a force field, protecting them from all harm.

"I trust her, and I want to build a sisterhood with her," Renee admitted. The words came out scratchy and on edge, but true nonetheless.

Julian gave the door a once-over. He remembered the voice that belonged to a new long-lost sister. He replayed her tone and searched for her personality within it. They were almost destroyed twice by sisters of Renee's, and if the saying "three times the charm" held any truth, then any ill intentions on Madison's end would cause their world to crumble.

"Say something," Renee pushed. She understood why Julian's words now either fell short or came out far and few between, but she needed to have this conversation. It was her last chance at a family, and the only way she saw that happening was if Julian agreed.

"You know what I'm thinking, Renee."

"Still, tell me." Renee knew his thoughts, yet hearing them would help her determine whether letting someone new in their life was the right thing to do.

"You want to dive right back into what pulled us all apart? We're still on shaky legs and in the process of healing. Concentrate on us."

"I am. That's why if you tell me you don't approve, it won't happen. But I have to tell you how I feel. I want to have at least one healthy relationship with someone in my family, so I have to take into consideration that there's a chance she may be the sister I might need."

"What else do I need to know about her?" Julian asked.

"Everything if she'll be around. But the most important thing you should know now is that she despises Carmen just as much as we do, and she is just as hurt and lost as me." After she spoke, Renee sat up to look directly at Julian.

"So, you can relate to her."

Renee nodded her head.

"Fine, but one fuck up, one indication that she's a relative of Carmen's, and she's gone."

Renee smiled, the truth in his words apparent and understood on her end.

"I promise." She kissed his cheek, her hand rubbing the right side of his face. "Now, let's go meet her."

It had been a long time since Madison cooked a meal for anyone except herself. She kicked herself for entering Renee's room without knocking, yet she looked at it from a positive perspective. Now she knew how much food to make.

The pots and pans sizzled with breakfast as she cracked an egg from its shell and dropped it into a pan. Madison turned the bacon off, the strips now hardened and brown. Cut fruit sat in a bowl while she waited for the hash browns, sausage, and pancakes to cook. While organizing the plates on the island, which resembled a buffet, she remembered the orange and cranberry juice she'd placed in the freezer. She retrieved it along with drinking glasses, and she set the table. Checking on the rest of the food on the stove, it hit her. Did she make too much? According to the clock, it was technically lunchtime, but since they'd slept in late, Madison tried to play catch up and show her appreciation for Renee's hospitality.

Dressed, and with peaceful looks washed on their faces, Renee and Julian found their way into the kitchen. "Madison, you didn't have to cook." Renee looked at the spread, reminiscing on how far she used to take it when cooking for company.

"I know. It's a thank-you for letting me stay." Madison turned off the stove and put the remaining food on separate plates.

"Madison, I want to introduce you to Julian."

Madison couldn't hide it. The surprise she felt reflected in her big eyes. She'd heard so much about Julian, but she didn't expect to meet him so soon. After wiping her hands off on a rag covered with stitching of rolling pins, seasoning bottles, and spatulas, she held out her hand. "Nice to meet you."

Julian took her hand, shook it, and released it within seconds. He never spoke, only nodded his head.

This was Renee's first time eating at her kitchen table. Since moving in, she either ate out or took her food with her into her room, so sitting here was a nice change of setting. For the first few moments, no one exchanged words. They only ate, a newcomer changing the dynamic of things.

Julian was the first to finish his meal. He wiped his mouth with a thick golden napkin and stared at Madison until she returned his glare. However, Madison concentrated on her dish. And when she finished, she dropped her fork, only to look up and see that Julian and Renee had finished their meals. Madison then took it upon herself to stand and clear the table.

"That will be taken care of," Julian voiced. His hand signaled for her to sit back down. Placing her empty cup and dirty napkin on her square plate, she sat down.

"First, I would like to thank you for the meal and let you know that it was good," Julian began.

It was now Madison's turn to remain tight-lipped and nod her head.

"But you didn't come here to cook, so tell me, what do you want?" The saying "fool me once, shame on you, fool me twice, shame on me" played in Julian's head. Making the same mistake twice would never be their reality again.

"You think I have a motive, like Carmen."

"I think exactly that. Now, if you and Renee spoke for as long as she says you did last night, then I take it you know quite a few things about us."

"You don't scare me. If that's what you're trying to sell me, I'm not buying it." She knew where this conversation was headed, and part of Madison was jealous. Never had she had a man defend her, only humiliate and degrade her when she didn't acknowledge his entrance into the club. She had yet to meet her knight in shining armor.

"I don't work off fear. I work off facts and promises. Now tell me some facts, and I'll make you some promises."

Renee waited for Madison's response. Madison saw Renee's and Julian's hands clasped together under the table. *It must feel good to be loved,* she thought.

"I have no motive up my sleeve. And if I did, I would have put my plan in motion a long time ago. I knew about Renee for years," Madison confessed.

Julian looked at Renee. He had no idea she was aware of Renee's existence before they even knew Madison's name.

"I didn't come looking for Renee. I didn't expect to even meet her. But now that I have, I want to get to know my sister. I don't have any family left."

"And how do you feel knowing that one of the reasons death has hit your family is because of us? How can you build a relationship with the person whose friends are behind it?"

Maybe Madison was a monster, because the answer she was preparing to give still sat right with her since she first felt it. "Because I don't care. None of this would have happened if it weren't for Carmen and her fucked-up ways, but then again, my family had been fucked up since the beginning of time. What do you want me to do? Seek revenge? Slither my way into Renee's life, and make you all pay one by one? Then what would I be doing? Nothing but continuing a cycle that only proved to be destructive for people who barely even cared about me. I'm done. I just want to be happy and live life the best way I can, even if it means breaking bread with murderers." Madison balled her hands into fists, willing her gumball-sized tears away. "Now make me a promise," she challenged.

"Zeke is dead, Madison. That same little boy who followed you around as a child is dead. The person we put on the job never misses," Renee admitted. She needed Madison to understand what she was doing.

"I tried talking him out of it, but he made his bed, so now he must die in it." Tears dropped, and when they did, Renee and Julian squeezed each other's hand.

"You bring any harm her way, and I promise you I'll kill you," Julian warned.

Wet faced, Madison smiled and said, "Good to know."

Chapter 26

John Legend's "All of Me" circulated through the modern home dipped in darkness. The living room curtains danced as the wind trespassed and forced its way through the open window. Stillness invaded the foodless, sparkling-clean kitchen as a drop of water threatened to fall from the sink's faucet, hanging in the balance. The droplet held on for dear life as its liquid physique stretched low, then snapped back up.

The second-floor hallway floorboards and bare walls squeaked. Its creaks and old interior moved with the wind and spoke in the night. The bathroom performed magic tricks, the lights flickering on and off, then randomly blinking at an unreliable, unpredictable tempo. The bedroom held the most dreadful sense of serenity. Its loss of romance suffocated the air and tore away at reality. A flat, even surface occupied the right side of the bed. Its perfectness brought attention to the dip on its neighboring side. It should have never been that well kept, even leveled, or maintained. It should have been ruffled, scented with perfume, and sprinkled with love. Renee should have been there. She should have been his bed partner and the warm body he melted into, but she wasn't, because she was too busy falling into waterfalls with Julian.

After Jared killed Zeke, he drove straight to a hotel in Staten Island. He avoided his home after a kill. He craved to see Renee and celebrate what she asked for him to do, but he couldn't. If he was being followed, he refused to lead anyone to his queen. So he waited and locked himself away, suppressing the urge to call and text Renee. He waited until sunrise on a Saturday morning while the rest of the world remained in bed to check out. After stopping by his home, his car took him to Renee's. Anxious to see her, his hands shook while controlling the steering wheel. Pulling into her driveway, he stepped out of his vehicle and inhaled the fresh air.

In search of the only person tolerant enough to deal with him and tainted enough to understand him, he skipped steps to make it to his love. His new mission was to make it to her as fast as he could. Inside her room, nothing was different or outside of Renee's personality. Nothing except for the bathroom door being wide open and exposing her and Julian's lovemaking. Jared's heart stopped, eyes blurred, and legs wobbled. His comfort zone was stolen, and he was locked away in a land of heartbreak.

Jared felt his heart giving out. The sensual touches, bites on the skin, whispers in Julian's ear, and heavy releases of breath validated what Jared was missing, what Renee never gave him and saved for Julian. Their bodies clicked together like puzzle pieces snapping into place. Her facial expression was a painting on an easel, captured by an artist. Her body formations emulated undiscovered flexibilities and struck a jealous chord within Jared's soul.

His boots took a step farther in the water, his firearm in his hand and just as alert and visible as he. However, the danger slapped in front of the two lovers went unnoticed. Their love was blind, and it canceled out anything surrounding them. Jared raised the gun, pointing it directly at the side of Renee's temple. He pictured himself blowing her brains out, but when he imagined her body hitting the bathroom floor, his need to murder vanished. This was not a life he could take. He could not add another lover to his chain of kills. This woman meant too much to him. Jared lowered his gun. With it still exposed, he walked out of the house slowly with his heart ripped out of his chest.

At Jared's dreary, loveless home, Jared's favorite gun and six bullets sat on a circular table once dusty and cloudy and now cleaned to perfection. One by one, Jared loaded the gun with each of the bullets. Only one would do the trick, but a game of Russian roulette was not in his plans. Jared pushed the final bullet inside the weapon, and his eyes clung to the picture of Renee on the table.

Tears rolled and tumbled down Jared's face, moisturizing his skin for the last time.

"I pray the Lord my soul to take." Jared's prayer broke the silence, his heartfelt words filling God's ears and taking His hand. Jared's blurry vision held on to the portrait of Renee. He pointed the gun to the right side of his head, and one last tear splashed against the table.

"Amen."

Chapter 27

Carmen selected one of the many cabs awaiting passengers at the entrance of the hospital and jumped inside. Proud and feeling accomplished, she rattled off the address to the new hotel where she would now lay her head and meet up with her luggage. Courtesy of Detective Reynolds, her belongings were transported to the establishment and the bill for her stay paid. Carmen pushed the slanted-styled glasses farther up her nose and watched as New York's architecture rushed past. She was in a state of admiration. Her thoughts rewound to the manipulation she exercised on the detectives and psychiatrist.

Being a prisoner of a mental institution and unaware of the possible protection it would supply was not a desire of Carmen's. She wanted out and the ability to finish what she started. Her acquaintance with the cat in her dream sparked the need for survival and supplied her with everything needed to keep her from seeing the inside of a psych ward. Carmen was very manipulative when meeting with the psychiatrist. Her words were well thought out, filled with emotion, and believable. It didn't help that the doctor was new to this profession and a gullible young'un who ate everything Carmen was feeding her.

"I should become a psychiatrist," Carmen whispered. Her education took a backseat to her need for a man to care for her. Her intelligence was never a problem. Her goals and lack of independence had led her into an unstable, easily deleted position. Both sisters chased after their education, and although Renee was the only one who finished her time in a classroom, disappointment filled Carmen over not even attending college. Carmen was using her wits for all the wrong reasons, and only God knew where she would be now had she used them for good.

Carmen dropped her head back on the worn leather seat. Her body rocked with the car as it made a sharp left and drove them into a large, dimly lit alley surrounded by nothing but space and a large building. Not even the sunlight lightened its mood. The cab sat at a red light, where she caught a glimpse of a group of women entering a building. It was the early afternoon, and by the looks of the building they entered, the establishment was closed. One by one, the young ladies draped in tight clothing and loud accessories disappeared inside, the lurid sound of the heavy metal door closing behind them. Carmen sat up, the words, *Madison's job,* popping in her head. The car took off, and the large building shrunk in size.

"Change of plans," she told the driver. "Take me to Long Island."

Carmen sat in the car staring at the home she used to visit as a child, the home she wished she could visit more since they couldn't bring her sister home.

The cab driver sat there quietly. No music filled the silence, and instead of listening to instruments and vocals, he listened to the afternoon's breeze. The meter was running, so why complain and rush her? The time Carmen used reminiscing and looking out the window gave him a moment's peace.

The quietness and stillness the home gave off made her see that she wanted her family. Lying in that hospital caused random thoughts to swarm, twist, and turn inside of Carmen's mind. One of those thoughts was if she had died, no one would have cared, and no one would have been concerned enough to hold a funeral for her.

Everyone who loved her was dead, and those who weren't had thrown her into a sea of isolation. Being in close proximity to sisters she had no dealings with, other than violence, was not a healthy life to live. There was no bettering her relationship with Renee, but Carmen hoped there was still a chance with Madison. Things didn't go right the last time they spoke, but Carmen was a believer that time healed all wounds. In due time, Madison would come to her senses and speak with her once more. Madison's sharp words and forward attitude had pain labeled all over them. She was a hurt creature who had always looked for a way out but could never outsmart the cage her emotions had placed her in. Now all Carmen had to do was be vulnerable and honest. All she had to do was be human and begin the process of building a relationship with her sister. Madison did nothing to her, and all she wanted was to be a part of the family their parents forced apart.

Carmen removed the shades from her eyes, repairing what had been damaged before her birth required her to come in plain sight: no hidden agendas, no manipulations, just her. She slapped money into the driver's hand, and as the door slammed, she heard him tell her, "Good luck." He knew nothing about the problems of her life, or the thoughts in her brain, but he knew the sight of pain and nervousness. He knew the battle within and what it felt like to have to right what had been wronged for so long. A small, timid smile graced her face while she speed-walked to the front door.

Ringing the doorbell, she brushed her fingers across her cheeks, her makeup terribly missed. The need to cry flourished and scratched at her. There was but so much wrong a person could do before they broke down and just wanted to be loved. She rang the doorbell several more times, then turned to knocking when no one answered.

She looked out at the neighborhood, unaware of whether she should make her way to the club in case no one answered. Carmen didn't know where Madison lived. She chose not to obtain that information after finding out about the life her sister lived, but now that she stood outside in the cold for the second time, she wished she'd gotten the address. In the middle of her admiring the home across the street, the front door finally opened. Carmen looked at Roy. His heavy eyes, ruffled hair, and alcohol-spewing pores told the tale of dismay. Carmen froze momentarily, unsure of how to react.

"I was meaning to come visit you in the hospital, but I've been a little busy." Roy reached over to the side of the door, and when he returned, he had a bottle of whiskey in his hand. It had a few sips left, and by the look in Roy's eyes, he would eliminate it if it was the last thing he did. Instantly, Carmen's heart dropped.

"When did you get out? Did you give the police a description of the bastard who did this to my son? Is it that same motherfucker from the funeral?" Although his appearance said one thing, Roy spoke very evenly paced. The poison he took, which normally slurred speech and sprinkled forgetfulness over heads, seemed weakened by Roy's system.

Catching herself staring, Carmen came out of her thoughts and answered, "I got out this morning, and yes, I told them who it was. But it wasn't the guy from the funeral. It was someone associated with him."

Roy nodded his head. Carmen wanted to go inside, but the conversation continued where she stood. Roy balanced himself by holding on to the frame of the door and taking light sips of the dark liquor. "Good. I hope they get that son of a bitch. They took my life away."

Carmen turned away, unable to look the man in the face, let alone the eye. Her posture turned rigid and uneven. Uncomfortable, she asked, "Is Madison here?"

Roy finished off the remainder of the bottle, threw it out on the lawn, and disappeared inside the house. Wide open, the door swung on its hinges. When Carmen was unable to see him, she cautiously walked inside. An alarming smell hit her nose, forcing her attention on the four-day-old fruit flies swarming around. Carmen quickly closed the door behind her, applied her sunglasses to her eyes, and remained where she stood. She couldn't do it. Looking Madison in the eye and stripping away the fake was one thing, but watching Roy crumble and break was something else. Roy reappeared with a bottle of scotch in one hand and vodka in the other. He walked around with them proudly. Making a turn into the living room, he flopped down on the couch, his feet bumping into one another.

"Excuse the mess," he announced, and without a second passing after his apology, he knocked old containers, dishes, and napkins off the table. A combination of food and unfinished liquor smashed together and created a village known as a mess on the floorboards. "You can't take a seat? It's okay. There was once a time when your ass couldn't have a seat because you were always pouncing around when you came to visit your sister." Noticing he only had the bottles of liquor on the table and no cups, Roy shrugged his shoulders, popped the scotch open, and introduced his lips to the brim of the glass bottle. "Want some?" he asked. His arm stretched out, the bottle swaying from side to side.

Carmen heard his question but paid it no mind. Her eyes roamed around the home. Taking in all the details that remained from her childhood, added fixtures reminded her of what they'd replaced. The floors were now glazed brightly by a buffer. However, that did nothing to hide the deep scratch she put in the floor, the scratch Madison told Prue and Roy was her doing.

The view she had of the kitchen allowed her to discover that it had been remodeled with updated gadgets and colored walls. She searched for the pan Prue used to make her famous fried chicken. Her insides became wrecked when she didn't immediately spot it but eased when its worn, faded outer shell peeked out from behind one of the other pans hanging over the kitchen island.

Carmen looked at the ceilings, then up at the windows. *Home.* This place read home and was where her best family-filled memories lay. Roy sat, looking around, occasionally drinking and falling victim to his memories. Eventually, Carmen stepped inside the living room, her black sneakers dodging the spoiled food soaked in liquor. Beside the fireplace, she took a seat and relaxed herself.

"She's not here," Roy finally answered.

Snapping her neck in his direction, Carmen remembered the question she asked long ago.

"But she won't be coming back." The taste of scotch began to bore him, so he switched to vodka. The instant a drop entered his system, his sight began to blur, and his reflexes slowed. Roy could handle a lot of alcohol, but everyone had a limit. Roy just wasn't willing to recognize his.

"Why? What happened?" Carmen demanded to know. Her calmness was ripped away and now plagued with questions.

"She saw no use in seeking revenge against the people who took my family away. Therefore, without your mother and aunt around, I saw no use for keeping her in this family."

Discomfort settled further inside Carmen's bones. It wasn't until this moment that Carmen understood her sister's emotions. "How could you do that?" She forced out her words, soft and airless.

However, Roy heard nothing. He heard only the sound of the liquor swooshing back and forth the more he moved it around. "She'll be okay. Looks like she found a friend in the girl next door when I sent her packing. Let Renee deal with her shit. It was ridiculous that she still had a room here anyway. We should have made it a playroom for Zeke's kids when we had the chance," Roy confessed, unaware of the information he divulged.

The saliva coating Carmen's throat ran dry, and her concern for Madison withered away. "What did you say?"

"The girl next door. She seemed to have gotten in good with her. I saw her going into her house the night I kicked her out. Her name is Renee. Zeke was doing business with her. She was a friend of your aunt's." The weight of Roy's head was now increasing, and his neck strength was weakening. Gone were his strong presence and small indications that he was inebriated. His posture was now slouching, and his head drowned in the soft couch.

"How does she look?" Carmen screamed. This couldn't be happening. Her secret, the card she pulled to hurt Renee, could not have been back to haunt her. It would have been too big of a coincidence that Renee was Prue's neighbor.

Roy's eyes were now closed and easing into sleep. Yet before he gave himself over fully to rest, he told her, "Like you." It was the perfect ending to Roy's days of drinking and lack of sleep. Since his son's death, no peace was delivered to him, and drinking was his only comfort. He fell asleep, and before he fully had the chance to rest his body, the sounds of a car starting up sounded outside.

Carmen jumped out of her seat and rushed out the door. A dark vehicle turned out of Renee's driveway and sped off, the silhouette of two heads in the front seats heading toward the city.

Chapter 28

"So this is the infamous strip club?" Renee asked. She looked at the club Madison was recently fired from through the tinted window of her automobile. "You couldn't have picked a better spot to shake your ass?"

The question was offensive and unneeded, but stationed outside the building and looking at it, Madison understood why it was asked. It wasn't how it used to be. Back in the day, it used to be better. After management changed and Madison was hired, the club obtained its fifteen minutes of fame due to celebrity sightings and the club's elaborate decor, but eventually, the club's time in the limelight ended. The once-hot place to be was becoming old and predictable. Now Madison's place of employment was a run-down building sitting on a street whose value had plummeted.

Madison looked at herself in the rearview mirror and saw that the young girl who started out in that place was gone. She detected a wrinkle or two forming and the sadness in her eyes begging for happiness. It was then that Madison asked herself, *what am I doing? When will I grow up?* Depressed by that realization, Madison reminded herself that this was not the time for her to self-analyze, so she put on a brave face and faced Renee. Trying to lighten up her mood, she replayed in her head what Renee had asked, and laughed.

"Shut up. Back in the day, I made this place popping."

Renee chuckled, the laughter a temporary relief from Madison's reality. Renee looked at the club, then back at Madison. "Why are we here? Are you having second thoughts?" she asked.

Madison tried to be strong, tried to appear unbothered. "No," she lied.

"You're lying." Renee smirked. "You don't want to do this. It will take a lot more than someone terrorizing you for you to set out to harm them, now won't it?"

Madison felt Renee's stare relax on the side of her face and numb her skin.

"You don't have to be what you think you should be." Listening to Madison talk and replaying conversations they'd had, Renee had already labeled her personally. The more Madison hurt, the more she tried to toughen up. However, with each attempt, she fell short of what she aimed to feel and tried to accomplish. Madison's heart went unprotected, and she tried to build a solid wall around it, but no brick stood tall. It only sat up straight for a second, then fell into pieces. Madison's anger was diluted by love and peace. She wanted to be angry, wanted payback, but she couldn't go through with it.

Looking at Madison, Renee could see that negative, vindictive actions were not her style. It seemed right at the time, only because the idea of being disrespected never sat right with Madison, but when it came down to it, her heart got the best of her.

"Would you think any less of me if I told you that you are right, and not only was I having second thoughts, but third and fourth thoughts?" Madison asked. Her question was drenched in emotion, yet her face held none. Madison wished she could stand by anger toward her coworkers, but her soul fought against such things after a certain amount of time. Madison had her moments when she was strong, but then her conscience would take over, and the need for peace would lead her to turn a blind eye.

The club was never their destination. They were supposed to be driving to Madison's home, where she would pack her belongings and stay with Renee temporarily. With Renee and Julian back together, moving back to Manhattan was a go. His absence was the only thing keeping Renee from reentering her old home, which had yet to sell. It held years of misery, but it was home and Long Island a stranger.

That morning, the three had agreed that Madison should move in. She had no employment, and her and Renee's needs to get to know one another were high. Moving Madison into her own space would have been an easy and fast transition, but it wasn't something Renee wanted. She wanted to get to know the only family member she had left. Things were moving fast, but life was short, and Renee refused to miss out on it any longer. So they jumped inside the car and rushed to Madison's, where she'd pack her belongings, starting tonight.

But instead of being surrounded by boxes, Madison sat looking at the club she forced Renee to drive to. Her second thoughts appeared out of nowhere, but it had to be done. She thought the building's presence would help dictate whether getting revenge was right.

Renee shook her head. "No, I wouldn't." Renee knew that although they both lived lives parents taught their children to steer clear of, her occupation was the reason almost all her humanity had been sucked out of her. Madison, on the other hand, still held on to what the girls at the club tried to terminate, and therefore she cared what people thought. "You talk a good game, but I understand that some people are not meant to sit in the stands, let alone play the game."

They were one of those pair of sisters who were opposites. There would be times when the youngest would act as the oldest, and the eldest would sit back and follow her lead. Renee started the car, preparing to leave the club behind.

"Why can't I do it? Why can't I be like you?" Madison looked at her sister. When she found out she was fired, she dared Renee to prove the clout she held by helping her handle her strip club enemies. And now here she was backing away from a challenge she put out.

Renee pulled her car out of its spot and laughed. Never had anyone told her they wanted to have her personality. "That's funny, because I wish I were like you." Renee wished she could move on from issues without reacting to each one like Madison had chosen to do, but before she tried achieving that goal, she had to do one more thing: a favor to Madison.

Without the heart to seek revenge, but instead wanting to move on with life and do what was right, Renee wanted to be Madison, and that alone was an accomplishment. Never would it be a reality, because Renee didn't let go of things, and that included Madison's torment from her coworkers.

Renee dropped Madison at her soon-to-be ex-home and took the long way back to Long Island, the landmarks and smell of New York restaurants a rejuvenating experience. Over an hour later, she pulled into her driveway, where she sat and acknowledged her home's elegance and lack of comfort. This place wasn't for her. She couldn't build on a foundation that held no history. She had to go home. Entering the quiet environment, she sought out the only familiarity those bricks contained. Renee locked eyes on the body lost in cotton sheets and blankets hibernating and regaining energy in her bed.

Like a lion zeroing in on its prey, Renee approached Julian slowly and with ease, her movement thought out and with the grace of a ballerina. Quietly and without disturbance, she pulled herself onto her large, high bed, her knees sinking into the mattress and shaking her balance. Renee's head lowered and lips parted, her teeth grabbing hold of the comforter. With rough, powerful tugs, she tore it from his body.

Julian's position in the bed did not alter. Instead, he remained in a deep sleep, unaware of his surroundings. Now on top of him, Renee had her prey under her claws and pinned to the bed. Her hands traveled over her hometown and visited her favorite locations. The slow movements erupting from his body meshed with hers. His eyes remained shut; however, his physique participated in the love affair and grew more intense with every touch of her lips and feel of her breath cooling off the internal temperature after every kiss.

Renee had never stepped foot inside of a strip club. It was never a thought that ran through her head, or a spur-of-the-moment entertainment activity she set out to accomplish. It was just a place she knew was there, but saw no need to indulge herself in. It was a place that lost souls inhabited and money controlled. It was a stale, neon-colored, music-filled room on which attention was placed during the weekends then forgotten about once life rolled back around on Monday. Renee would have never gone there, but for her sister, she'd go once.

In boots and a ski jacket, Renee's attire weighed her down and forced her to stand out in a room where clothing was minimal and easily removable. Yet she walked across the room, which flashed with color and reeked of lust, toward the bar, with the bottom of her boots adding to the bass the speakers let out. Insecure, questionable looks given to her from employees were motivating. Her covered body acquired the attention of customers whose vision was normally cast on flesh in bits and pieces of fabric. The strippers danced in slow motion, and their facial expressions hardened as she walked by. No man complained about the lack of movement given by the women, because they, too, were lost in the trance of the beauty walking by. Each low-eyed scowl Renee received was dropped in her memory bank, a sleek smile etching itself across the left corner of her lips. Madison had no friendships here. The ivory to her ebony had left, leaving no one for Renee to overlook.

Renee took the seat of a man at the bar who got up. He was marching hand in hand with a towering dancer with high cheekbones. The name "Ms. Russia" was stitched across the bottom of her shorts. They walked toward a metal door in the back of the club. A clean napkin sat beside a half-drunken beer, and Renee used it to wipe down her seat. She watched the bartender give head bobs to customers surrounding the bar and maneuver from man to woman, woman to man in that exact equation before turning to her. The shock in his eyes and decrease in his steps told her hello before his mouth ever got the chance. The sweat leaking from the beer bottle fell on his hand and woke him up, alerting him of the gentleman two seats down from Renee, who put in his order nearly five minutes ago. He delivered the beer, collected the cash, and ignored the rest of the men determined for a drink.

"Jordan," Russell whispered.

The day he stopped working for Renee appeared in his thoughts, and he skimmed through every possibility as to why she would be here. His break from the illegal life was a smooth and painless one. It was a life he could no longer commit to. It was a phase in his youth he saw his way through, so when he sat down with Renee and explained this to her, the woman who literally took him off the street and gave him work when his abusive father kicked him out understood.

The desperation his brown eyes were lined with when Julian introduced him to her was unforgettable. He was 14 and naive to it all. Renee did nothing to fully contaminate his mind, except to make him her lookout when dirty deeds were done and occasionally deliver packages. He was no solider, not a killer or beast who could survive in the streets. He was a kid and still a kid when he made his exit at the age of 20. So when Russell asked to sever all ties and leave on good terms, Renee respected that and wished him luck in his new life.

For some time after Russell's departure, things were good for him. He saved the money he made from Renee and enrolled in college. After graduating, he put his energy into becoming a sports agent, which made life not only remarkable, but unmanageable. The money this young man was making and the attention he was receiving from gold-digging women whose goal was to slide next to his athletic clientele pushed him into a world of sex. The lifestyles of the rich and famous destroyed him more than Renee's business could have ever done. The partying stole his attention, and he focused on the fast women lost in his pants. Business was no longer being handled, and bills were no longer paid. He was relapsing into poverty. It wasn't long before Russell was blacklisted and found himself bartending for one of the married women he lusted after. That was years ago, and although he was kicked out of the glitz and glam, he held on to the sex and screwed every woman who came his way. The only difference now was the women he slept with were no longer groupies, but drunks.

"How are you, Russell?"

Russell swallowed, wishing she had asked anything except for that. How could he tell the person who helped him up when he was down that life took him to new heights after leaving her, and that the power of the pussy led him back down lower than where he'd started? The glass a stripper slammed on the counter while rushing to the stage gave him a reason to divert his attention from Renee. He grabbed the glass and proceeded to work.

"I'm good. I'm good," he stuttered, his back turned. He finally took orders. Renee nodded her head and looked over his appearance, his skinny exterior telling her otherwise. The lies he told fell on well-informed ears.

"Then you have the energy to do one more job for me."

The lights cut off, and an alarm screamed. Red beacon lights lit the room, and a number of individuals, men and women, flocked toward the stage. There was one night per week when special shows out of the norm were performed, and no one wanted to miss them. Only a few people remained at the bar, their minds in a world of their own and eyes randomly checking for the show to start. Russell served his last drink and took a second to himself. He welcomed the erotic shows the club scheduled, because while they took place, he could breathe.

"I gave that life up," Russell reminded her. He was leaning on the bar, whispering for only her to hear.

"But you didn't give up fuckin'?"

Applause broke loose when the owner of the club stepped on stage. Him repositioning his tie expressed his pride felt toward what he had in store, his smile ready to set the freaks loose. Renee had been keeping tabs on Russell, watching him to ensure the secrecy he promised regarding her and her business remained intact. Russell looked around, making sure no ears had swallowed what she said.

"Jim!" he called out across the bar at his coworker, trying his best to carry his voice over the loud music that now helped introduce the dancers. "I need you to cover my side of the bar for a minute!"

Jim smirked, his arms folded against his chest. He leaned against the interior of the bar. His eyes locked on the stage.

"Pocket my tips for the rest of the night. I don't give a fuck. Just watch the bar for a second!"

Jim nodded, his vision never parting from what was to come. Russell came out from behind the bar, and Renee followed suit. They met at the far-right side of the building at a payphone between the men's and women's bathrooms.

"What do you want?" he nervously asked.

"For you to do what you do best: fuck."

"What the fuc . . ." He caught himself. Disrespect would not be tolerated, and although he was no longer on Renee's payroll, he knew some things remained the same. "What does my sex life have to do with anything?"

"Everything, I need for you to release the beast and do a little burning for me."

Russell's heart melted into his shoes and created a puddle. Knowing his extracurricular activities was one thing, but his health status was a whole different realm. He cleared his throat, pushed aside the extent of her knowledge, and attempted to hear what her contorted mind had in store.

"You screw the women who terrorized Madison in front of me right here, right now, and I'll pay for all of your medical bills. You'll have the best medication there is for HIV. All you have to do is spread the love."

The duty that was placed in front of Russell scratched at his bones and pulled at his nails. Premediated murder, the spread of a killer his blood and semen held, was now

in high demand. Just five months ago, he was diagnosed
with HIV and sentenced to a death that could not be
delayed, simply because not enough bills with pictures
on them warmed his bank account. He needed an out,
help to survive, and once again, Renee was there to pick
up the pieces of his life in shambles. Questions about
Madison's work relationship with her coworkers and her
connection with Renee walked through his thoughts, but
they easily evaporated into images of life with financial
help. His quiet reaction, asking no questions, let Renee
know that he would work for what he needed.

A change of music slammed into the club. Four women
in transparent glow-in-the-dark costumes took the stage
and fed the hunger salivating from the mouths of men.
The stage glowed, and the bar lit up, both taking on the
color white, brightly lit like Times Square in the middle of
the night. The strippers started their dance of seduction.
Touches landed on skin, and after minutes of fantasies
being rewarded to the audience, two of the topless women
pulled four men from the crowd and onto the stage. An orgy
broke out, its surprising performance causing customers
to wipe their eyes in order to confirm that what they were
seeing was real. Screams and a rise of applause exploded
and conquered the music. The sight of sex and adrenaline
pumped fiercely. Bouncers sprinted toward the audience
and pulled men lacking self-control off the stage, their grip
on one girl's ankle snatched away. The energy spit onto the
platform, and the sexual vibes escaping rejuvenated the
girls and heightened the chosen men's sexcapade.

Girls who were not on stage idly walked around the
club, resentment internally brewing because they were
not picked for the night's events. Men who were not lost
in the crowd but comfortable on the old couches nursed
their drinks and absorbed the fresh air the separation
between them and the crowd created. Strippers in need

of an outlet massaged the shoulders of men who were not drowned in the show and started their own porn video at their seats.

"Which girls gave Madison problems?" Renee asked. The glow from the bar kissed her cheek.

Numb to what he had agreed to and would soon carry out, his lips clung to one another while he turned and looked at the stage, his stare answering Renee's question. The women Renee set her eyes on were covered in body fluids without a care in the world.

"Did you fuck them?"

He shook his head no. HIV was enough to put an end to his one-night stands and ease him away into a safe zone.

"When this"—Renee looked once more at the depressing act, closed her eyes, and shook her head—"*entertainment* is done, make it happen. Get them into one of those secluded rooms, and fuck them like you never fucked before."

Chapter 29

Money spoke loud to a man of greed. Russell was unable to finish his sentence, let alone tell his boss how much Renee was willing to pay to see him have sex with his top strippers, before he agreed. Sexually drained customers were scattered among the club with drinks in their hands while enjoying the everyday sets the women performed. The quiet, satisfied aura now taking place eased under the metal door located in the back of the club. The room Renee, Russell, and the four women determined to kick Madison off her stripper pedestal occupied was large, cold, and made up of stainless steel completed with cozy furniture and clean sheets. This room was set aside for high rollers and taken better care of than the rest of the establishment. Alcohol, cigarettes, and party drugs such as ecstasy in small red velvet boxes outlined the room. This free drugstore made employees wish for an invitation.

In the middle of the room sat a round glass table holding a drinking glass, with its matching decanter filled with a golden liquid in front of a high-backed cream chair. In the seat, Renee watched the youngest of the girls lying naked on the slippery sheets open her eyes when Russell removed himself from her only to see Renee watching their intimate moment.

Windy always had a crush on Russell. The friendly and delicate approach he had given her when she first entered the club made her feel like she had a friend. The drinks he supplied her with before her sets and back-room flings were 90 percent alcohol and 10 percent soda. Those drinks helped put her in the mind frame needed to function in the business and never stopped, even when their boss advised him to. There were times the owner wanted the girls sober. "No one wants sloppy pussy," was one of his favorite sayings, and at certain times he held the girls to those standards. But Windy needed drinks, and whenever Russell came across a drug that could take her away and make it possible for her to perform, he gave it to her free of charge.

She closed her eyes, waiting for him to once again enter her mine and drill for gold. He stuffed her breast inside his mouth and lifted his torso for stability when Emerald, a middle-aged Vietnamese woman obsessed with the color green, slipped her head underneath him and filled her mouth with his manhood. Pre-ejaculation seeped out of Russell and took comfort in the open wound lunged in her gums. The slight burning sensation its contact caused forced Emerald to shift his penis to the left side of her mouth and lap her tongue over its hole.

Happy for the gratification, he dove into Windy's lips and passionately made love to her mouth. Windy kissed Russell, hard, the need for love causing small birds with hearts in their mouths to spin above their heads. The intensity between the two tore down the sex-intensified room and hurt the plan Renee had set in motion.

Glitter and Whisper sat at the top of the bed watching, zoned out and, for the first time, the audience instead of the act. Renee was clear that there would be no girl-on-girl action, so while Russell was occupied, the last two strippers sat unsure of what part to play. Entertained by their lack of motivation to earn a buck, Renee grinned while shaking her head.

"Get to work, ladies. Your lack of teamwork is forcing money out of your pockets and back into mine."

Hearing they were in danger of losing money from the no-name woman, Glitter raced to the bottom of the bed and forced herself beside Emerald, where she would taste Russell's testicles. Glitter sparkled even in the brightly lit room. She drenched herself in the small, pretty paper because not many men liked the decoration. It was a tactic used to keep her on the stage where she felt most comfortable. Being an important asset to the club like Madison was highly significant to Glitter. However, Glitter chose to win her throne through the stage and not in the rooms.

Whisper, the most outspoken, who taunted Madison most, whispered sweet nothings in her john's ears, staring at the bed's arrangements, her eyebrows sinking in. Renee could see just by how Whisper looked on that she was an intimidator. She was a wordsmith who manipulated others and could never fall in line but led the pack.

So slowly and on her own time, Whisper slid next to Windy and Russell and broke their kiss. Grabbing him by his hair, she lifted his head and ravished him with kisses of her own. The bed became a sex battlefield where Glitter's and Emerald's heads knocked together like a game of Ping-Pong. The awkward position of Russell's body and the pulling of his genitals created discomfort mixed with the need for more. The deprivation of appetite in Russell's kisses alerted Whisper to his discomfort, and her eyes searched for the cause. Glitter and Emerald pushed at one another. Saliva dripping from the corners of their mouths and landing on the new rug alerted Whisper that the pulling of his skin was taking the fun out of her job.

Whisper pulled her foot back and kicked each woman in the forehead. One by one, the force pushed Glitter and

Emerald off the bed and on their behinds. The intensity the room encountered after both women hit the floor nearly put a dent in the walls. Whisper pulled Russell off of Windy, his body landing on top of hers while she fell on her back next to Windy. The little bit of drugs she consumed upped her strength, Supergirl in the flesh.

Russell slid right inside of her. Whisper committed herself to the act of physical contact and contracted her vagina walls, determined to squeeze and massage all that he had from him. The show involving five turned into two, and everyone's gaze fell on Windy. There wasn't one dancer in the building who wasn't aware of her budding love for Russell.

From the floor, still in shock over being literally kicked to the side, Glitter and Emerald stared at Windy, their hearts beating radically and thoughts doing jumping jacks. Renee smiled. She knew the look of infatuation and borderline puppy love when she saw it. She focused on how quickly Windy undressed and fell into Russell's arms the instant they waltzed inside the room. She was competing for his attention and thought if he had a taste of her first, he would ignore the others.

The same women who pulled together against Madison were now crumbling among themselves. They saw Madison as the enemy, and now that she was gone, they'd replaced her with one of their own. Renee set out for revenge on behalf of Madison, but she had no idea the experience would be so entertaining, so emotional. She laughed. Karma had come full circle, and she had front-row seats. The echo of the embarrassing and judgmental snicker escaping Renee's mouth caught Windy's attention and asked her some questions.

You gonna let her take your man like that? You gonna let her outshine you? The questions boomed inside Windy's mental. Sitting up, she rested her hand on his shoulder in preparation of pulling him off Whisper when his body ran stiff and waves of satisfaction broke through his length. The enjoyment Whisper accomplished by causing him to ejaculate raced through her face and achieved eye contact with Windy. Her smirk alone caused desperation to rear its ugly head and Windy to pull Russell away from Whisper.

Like a doll, for the second time, Russell had been pulled off a female. However, this time he landed on his back, and Windy's mouth indulged in the cream releasing from his manhood. Semen tumbled out of Whisper's vagina, and a string of white followed Windy and Russell. Russell's body moved from left to right. The intensity of the oral sex became too much, and he fought against the exquisite feelings, yet held on to them tight. The fast nods Windy was performing was a work of art on a canvas called a bed.

Amused by Windy's aggression, Emerald and Glitter got back on the bed and held an antsy Russell down. Occasionally his hands tried pushing Windy's head away, so the moment Glitter noticed this, she pinned his arms down, and Emerald secured his legs. They wanted him to feel every inch of pleasure pulsating through his body without interruption.

No longer limp from his prior release, Russell sat heavy in Windy's mouth. The building of round two climbing up his manhood sent him into a rage. He snatched his arm away from Glitter, grabbed Windy by her jet-black waves, and pushed himself deeper into her throat. Erupting, his hot lava splattered itself inside her mouth. Sperm filled Windy's cheeks, and with two big gulps, she swallowed it whole.

Russell looked at the wall. So much had been pent up from the last few months, and the second he finally released himself, he felt free. However, now that his body was at ease, he was haunted by his dirty deeds. His irresponsible ways had just affected a good two out of the four women he was sent after. There was a chance the virus didn't cling to them, but Russell knew the truth. He could already see the death sentence in their eyes.

The females laughed at Russell's exhaustion. The rise and fall of his chest and the excessive sweat made him look as if he had lost weight. He searched the silver ceiling for reassurance that what he was doing was right, but nothing showed.

Renee stood. The decanter was hardly empty, yet she chose to taste new liquor. She walked past Russell, his head comfortably on the mattress when he felt the palm of her right hand tap his cheek three hard, quick times.

"You have another round in you, don't you? These two beautiful ladies haven't had the pleasure to make your acquaintance." She smiled, her eyes landing on Glitter and Emerald, who were now tucked away in a corner next to a coffee table, snorting the drug of their choice. The high rollers room gave the strippers unlimited access to poison, and all they had to do was sell their bodies.

Russell turned away. His head's movements caused a drop of sweat to moisturize Renee's hand before pulling away and heading to the liquor. Whisper sat up, her breast free and her layered bronze hair giving off static. Wrinkles filled her face, and her body stiffened as she saw the proud look smothering Windy's face. Her face scrunched up.

"You look like someone I know," she told Renee. Her lips firmly locked together, and her eyes tightened.

"Oh, really? Then I guess she's a ravishing beauty in a house of disaster. A force to be reckoned with."

"I wouldn't say that," Whisper shot back.

Heading back over to the bed, Renee leaned down to Whisper's level. This would be the first and only time she stooped so low as to reach someone beneath her, the tips of her hair grazing Whisper's cheek.

"You look a little dried up, my dear. Have a drink." Renee flicked her fingers in Whisper's face, the sweat she had accumulated from Russell's cheek thrown in Whisper's face. Whisper turned to avoid the perspiration. However, one droplet landed on her lip. Renee smiled and wiped her hand on her jeans. Never had she been happier to have not relieved herself of someone's sweat the second it touched her.

Holding back her cutting words, Whisper forcefully wiped off the sweat Velcroed to her lip. This woman had the same cocky attitude as Madison, and because of that, Whisper's temper only worsened. Glitter eased herself beside her coworker when Renee walked away, her long dark legs on top of Whisper's.

"Calm down. She's paying more money than any other low-life who strolled in this shit hole," Glitter whispered. "Don't fuck this up for us."

Whisper violently pushed her flunky's legs off of her.

"Break time is over, ladies and gentleman!" Renee announced.

Russell tensed up. He didn't want to continue, but he had no choice. Half the deed, if not more, was already done.

"You two, get in there." Renee snapped her fingers at Glitter and Emerald, pointing them in Russell's direction.

Dazed in a corner and constantly snorting with her head laid back, Emerald finally achieved the high she had been waiting for. On all fours, she crawled to her victim, her toned shoulder blades popping out and showing off their definition. Her evenly filed nails clawed their way up the sheets, and like an animal, she crawled to him until she was directly on top of him. Her face exactly one inch from his, her green contacts stared him in the eye.

Joining the pack, Glitter crawled to the end of the bed, her long limbs out of the blue kicking Whisper in her thigh and wherever else her foot landed on her way to Russell. There was no way she wasn't getting her hit back before the night was over.

Swarmed with guilt-ridden thoughts, Russell pushed Emerald off of him and forced himself away from Glitter. If he was going to finish this, he was going to finish it under the influence. Hopping off the bed, he grabbed a red velvet box from the shelf on a wall containing two pills and a bottle of vodka sitting in a crystal bottle. The pills slammed into his tonsils and rushed down his throat after he downed as much liquor as he could.

The small capsules, which made him feel as if he were flying and carved a permanent smile into his face, kicked in after a few minutes. Uncontrollable laughter and happy moods took over. Russell jumped back on the damp bed and found himself positioned between Glitter's legs, his head diving into the waters of excitement. Moans and thunderbolts of desire ticked inside of her. An orchestra of moans sashayed throughout the room, drugs and liquor made everything okay. Windy admired Russell's physique from afar, and Whisper snorted the drug she couldn't afford.

Shivers and a strong release of fluids shot out of Glitter, the imagery spellbinding and mesmerizing. Russell fell on his back, inches from missing the bed, and Emerald's lips fell into his lap. The drug's control over her increased her strength and released the beast. Her teeth remained in attendance and, after seconds of slurps, scraped deep and hard into his flesh. The pain pushed Russell to sit up. However, the drugs numbed the pain and soothed it before he could truly experience the damage.

Once the shock wore off, Emerald showed her blood-stained teeth during her fit of laughter, the deep red bouncing off the room's light colors. Russell's groin was covered in blood, and although the sight alone was traumatizing to the average eye, these drug-induced individuals saw no harm in the wound. They saw it as them taking their antics to a new level. Common sense and human instincts were kicked to the side and an animalistic nature brought to the surface by the pills. Their eyes were clouded, and constant sweat adorned their foreheads, personalities shifted and consideration halted. They were no longer themselves, no longer on earth.

Savage tendencies took over, scenes from a vampire television show script were set in motion and gruesome at heart. Emerald continued what she started and seconds into it was interrupted by Glitter, who insisted on taking over. The room was moving. Russell's vision was contorted, yet he imagined himself on a quiet island while listening to the ocean, a world far from reality. After two minutes on the beach, Russell came back to the present. The present where all four girls he was hired to infect were now in the bed. Each woman catered to him orally, one after the other. When they were bored, they allowed his virus-filled erected tool inside their healthy interiors. It was a weapon no metal detector could discover, but it could still kill with one shot.

Renee watched, swishing around the untouched liquor in her glass. No head came up for air. No body disconnected from Russell's. It was another world they visited far, far from ours. Renee had her concerns. She wondered if the ploy she planned would succeed, or if luck would be with the women and keep them from catching Russell's illness. But as she watched the sexual acts continue, Whisper, who was now happy and carefree, and Windy, no longer territorial but willing to share, positioned themselves in such a compromising way that blood acted as their lubrication. Renee shifted her head

in an uncomfortable position, determined to see where
their positions ended and started. It was then, when a
cramp in her neck started to form, she knew her goal had
been accomplished.

Chapter 30

After watching people commit to sex for hours, it would be a long time before Renee watched another porno again. Whatever pills they absorbed turned them into never-ending freaks and boosted their energy by ten. No one noticed Renee leave the room, and no one heard the large bang when she opened and closed the door. Russell had fulfilled his job requirements, and now it was time she left. The club was back in full swing and more crowded than she remembered. Girls Renee didn't select to attend her special party watched her walk across the floor. Behind her, they searched for the girls who were considered the cream of the crop. Renee saw their looks and knew their questionable thoughts, but she continued to walk unbothered until one of them stopped her.

"Hi, excuse me, miss?"

Renee turned around, a small, timid, respectful voice calling for her attention.

"If you need someone else for another one of your parties, I'm available," she offered.

Renee looked at the girl. She was no older than 22, life still in her eyes and her innocence still intact. She smiled at her, the ugly side of this life not yet a reality to her.

"The party I had you don't want no part of, and by the looks of you, you don't belong here."

Renee walked away from the girl, leaving her words to settle in her mind and rethink whether the week she had been working at the club was really worth it. Reaching for the club's door, Renee's ears picked up on a conversation between two men who sat beside the exit, their table smothered with beers.

"Yo, you heard about Jared?"

"Jared . . . that name sounds familiar," said the old-school gangster whose tattoos told the story of his life on his neck. He tried to put a face to the name, and when he finally did, he looked back at the young stockbroker in shock.

"You talking about that hothead who works for Jordan?"

The young man nodded his head. "Dude's dead. On my way here I heard he committed suicide."

"Fuck outta here!" the OG screamed. He sat forward, his eyes wide. He was no longer interested in his drink.

Renee stood in the center of the doorway, her skin flushed with color. She looked at the men talking about Jared and told herself it was not true, that they had the wrong man in mind. But the more she listened to them speak, the more they confirmed they had the right person and that the pain she felt was justified.

Red, white, and blue beacon lights outlined the sky while sadness filled its interior. Mobs of civilians gathered around the tragedy-stricken home while uniformed individuals performed their duties. Discomfort stuck itself to the stale air, catering to the tinted windows of the vehicle Renee sat in, her clear brown skin now pale and saturated with horror. Voices seeping inside the cracked passenger's window became her informants.

Jared committed suicide. Beside his corpse sat a photo of an attractive woman no one had ever seen or at least remembered. For an hour, her seating arrangement had not changed, and although the chaos slowly dwindled away, Renee's thoughts remained in place along with her behind the wheel. Curious bystanders left the crime scene, their heads swaying from left to right and their mouths repeating details given by police. Finally, Renee was given a clear view of Jared's home, its firm-standing architecture overwhelming her. She had never been to his home, and now that it was in her sight, she didn't know how to feel. Her hand slid down the window, her last effort at having a connection with Jared. She was lost in the moment, and a knock against the window startled Renee. Pulling herself together, she rid herself of any emotions and looked out the window at Officer Reynolds.

Reynolds squinted, struggling to peer through the tint. He was shocked to see Renee's car at the scene and automatically approached the vehicle. Renee wiggled herself out of the driver's seat and, once secure, unlocked the doors with a push of a button, the clicking noise inviting Reynolds inside.

Reynolds flopped down in the seat. A defeated and agitated look was sprawled across his face. "Didn't expect to see you here, but since you are, know that you'll be receiving your up-front money back tomorrow morning. I just have to get it from my safe deposit box in Staten Island." Reynolds' tone was sour. Renee was paying him big money to lock Jared up, and now that Jared had disposed of himself, Reynolds would never see the additional $300,000 promised once the job was complete. And what made it worse was that Reynolds had spent the money that hadn't even touched his palms yet.

"Keep it," Renee mumbled.

Reynolds' eyebrows quickly rose in confusion. "Keep it?"

Changing the subject, Renee inquired, "The picture everyone's talking about, is it of me?" She never looked at Reynolds. Instead, she dedicated her stare to the world outside of the window.

"Yup." Reynolds stuffed his hands inside of his pockets. Never had he been so uncomfortable around a woman in his entire life. She was allowing him to keep $300,000 for starting a job he had not completed. This did not sit well with him and only made him question her ulterior motives.

"Besides you, does anyone else know or suspect that photo is of me?"

"Not at all, and if they do, it means shit now."

Dirty cops did dirty things, and stealing items from a crime scene was one of them. From his jeans pocket, Reynolds pulled out the photo and put it on the armrest between them. Slowly, he placed his hand inside his coat pocket instead of his jeans.

Snatching the picture, Renee folded it in two and stuffed it in her pocket.

"So, you're fuckin' Carmen?" This was the first time Renee looked at Reynolds. She had to, because she wanted to see the expression on his face when she questioned him and he forced lies to exit his mouth.

"I don't know a Carmen."

Renee nodded her head. "Really? Because a little birdie told me she was a witness in the Gibson murder."

Reynolds sat quietly. Questioning and catching criminals was what he was paid to do, but when it came to doing dirt, everything changed, including power being lost.

"With all due respect, what does my personal life have to do with you?"

"Everything, when that's the reason why the job couldn't get done."

Anger and guilt plagued Renee's soul. Unbeknownst to Jared, after he killed Zeke, he was supposed to not only take the fall for Zeke's murder, but also be thrown in jail for past crimes committed while working for Renee.

Renee had fallen in too deep when it came to Jared, and when she thought of how life would be once she went back to Julian, she saw nothing but turmoil. Jared would never let Renee go easily, so she had to put him away. He was a menace to society. Jared needed to be locked away like the animal he was and dwell in his element where the prison bars could act as a barrier between him and Renee.

However, nothing turned out that way. Things changed because of Carmen's presence at the crime scene, and although her finger pointing at Jared did nothing to derail Renee's plans, Reynolds' sudden infatuation with her threw things off course. Reynolds' inability to remain focused and move fast gave Jared the opportunity to slip between the cracks. The last thing she intended was for Jared not to be on this earth. She wondered what was on his mind and if he felt the shift in her feelings when she gave in to her heart and decided to venture back to Julian.

Although jail was a depressing fate on its own, Jared would have survived. To have thrown him in there replicated throwing a fish into water. He would have swum and become the king of his jungle. His separation from Renee would have given him strength, his anger would have fueled his survival, and now he could not even have that. Now the reason for his death sat beside Renee.

"You think I'm pussy whipped. You think I was busy concentrating on her instead of the task at hand. Whatever snitch you got feeding you this shit is a liar!"

"No, *you're* the liar."

Like Renee expected, Reynolds automatically became defensive. His eyes turned into a mixture of fear and anger—fear of the unknown and anger over getting caught. Quickly, he tore his gun out of his pocket and pointed it her way. However, the moment the barrel stared at her, bullets from her own gun tore into his face. Renee never blinked when skin, blood, and fragments of his face landed on hers. Her free hand never set out to move and wipe away the liquids and muscles. Instead, she just sat with her firearm still pointing his way. Reynolds' body fell into the window the moment a car drove by Renee's.

Outside movements barely existed. Only a few officers invaded Jared's lawn while others occupied his home. The silencer attached to the gun spit out whispers that easily went unheard. However, the orders being screamed from outside of the car were as loud as a stereo.

Renee pocketed her gun and pushed the body aside. Reynolds plummeted against the dashboard, no longer blocking her view of the police on Jared's lawn. Renee saw Day calling officers outside of the house in, and soon after, he told lingering bystanders to find their way home. Minutes later, when the night eased itself still and few people were around, Renee texted him. Moments after reading the message, Day walked over to Renee's car and signaled others near. It wasn't until he opened the car door that an undercover vehicle parked alongside Renee's car, blocking anyone's view of them. Stripping himself of his jacket and hat, Day threw them at Renee.

"Get out of here," he demanded, his attention everywhere.

In haste, Renee put on the oversized police jacket and hat, blood now hidden under law enforcement threads. With her hands jammed inside the pockets, she walked up the street, her head hung low. Once Renee was hidden in the dark, Day rushed to the car, blocking his deceased partner's body with his own. Giving him one last look, Day shook his head. *I tried to warn you.* Turning around, Day poked his head inside the undercover vehicle's rolled-down window and gave out instructions to the two men inside.

"Get rid of this shit," Day ordered, glancing over at Renee's car. "And after you do, go to Staten Island. There's three hundred thousand dollars in a safe deposit box for you to split. Here's everything you need to access it." Day took a notepad out of his back pocket and scribbled down an address and name capable of granting the officer access to Reynolds' cash. Ripping the page out of the miniature pad, he handed the rookie officer fresh out of the academy the information. He then watched as his retired comrade jumped inside the driver's seat of Renee's car and took off without looking back. The moment the tires drove into the night, the rookie was right on his tail, his second illegal activity within the last three days.

Day stood in the middle of the street, smiling and planning how he'd spend the money he gained from Reynolds' screw up.

Chapter 31

Renee's text message hitting Julian's phone pulled him from out of his sleep. It vibrated against the wood and forced his eyes to open and stare at it in annoyance. After a few minutes of trying to wake himself up, he reached for the phone and read her text sent to him hours ago.

It's done.

Without responding, Julian dropped the phone on the bed and turned around. He wasn't too sure how he felt about Renee eliminating Madison's problems. Renee was moving at the same quick speed she had moved when she met Carmen. She was using her power to better the lives of the sisters she had just met and knew nothing about. However, the conversation that took place between him, Renee, and Madison was enough for him to have a pinch of hope that Madison was different. She was now the light Renee had lacked and the motivation for her to believe in family.

Leaving his bed, Julian walked to the mirror and looked at his reflection. The stress that once filled his face was gone. Life now made sense, and he was complete now that Renee was back in his life. Curious as to when Madison would learn of the deed Renee had done for her, Julian stepped away from the mirror, his phone left behind. Time was winding down, and the sun was due to rise, so Julian headed downstairs, where he would wait for Renee. Her wanting to handle business on her own had him on pins and needles, but inside he knew all was well. Watching the idiot box, his mind drifted and relaxed.

A half-hour into a sitcom, the doorbell rang. He questioned who it was. Renee's house keys came into sight, and Julian smiled. Renee always managed to forget her keys. It was the exact reason he suggested she separate her car keys. The doorbell sent a loud echo to radiate throughout the house, summoning Julian to the door. Before he could open the door fully and get a look at his visitor, Julian was punched in the face.

Stumbling backward into the house, Julian moved his feet faster than need be, buying time until he could focus on the person in front of him. Dropping his hand from his face, he watched a drunk, wide-eyed Roy march in his direction. Julian's leaking lip splashed blood on the floor, and the feel of the thick liquid oozing from his flesh increased his temper and forced him to meet Roy halfway. The second Julian was within arm's length of Roy, Roy quickly swung. The first few swings missed, but when Roy increased his speed, he struck Julian in the side of his face.

Roy wouldn't stop swinging. Although he was intoxicated and struggled to remain balanced, his aim was accurate and unable to be stopped. Dodging every hit that he could, Julian was becoming restless. His bobbing and weaving and blocking whatever hits he could were slowly failing him. Roy's glossy, dull eyes remained fixated on Julian. When Julian caught the look of a man who would never stop until he was dead, he stopped avoiding his blows and rammed right into him, tackling him down. Roy flew off his feet, his back slamming against the floor.

By the shirt, Julian pulled Roy up and proceeded to repeatedly punch him in the face. After the first hit, blood erupted from Roy's nose. Crimson red splatted itself on

Julian's hands, withdrawing himself from reality. Julian allowed his fists to do the thinking and his survival skills to take the lead. With the tables now in Julian's favor, he ignored his surroundings and sank his fists deeper into Roy's face with every hit. His right fist was seconds from meeting Roy's face again when the shovel slapped him in his head. Falling backward, Julian's eyes shot open. All he remembered seeing was a rag coming toward him before knocking him out.

"You're moving in with someone you don't even know, and you're going now?" Nancy's face was scrunched up, and she fought to understand what she was hearing. One second Madison was out of work, and the next, she was moving in with her long-lost, rich sister. The information was head-scratching.

"She's my sister, and that's all I need to know."

Three hours had passed, and more than 50 percent of Madison's apartment had been boxed up. Sitting on the living room floor, she wrapped up vases and crystal knickknacks in bubble wrap. Her move was happening faster than she expected, and although she had no idea where this road would take her, she'd still get in the car.

Nancy watched the knickknacks her eyes always zeroed in on when visiting Madison's home become covered. Nancy had a lot she wanted to ask, but for some reason, while watching what she thought were permanent fixtures in Madison's home move off their shelves, she only asked a few.

"What about work? Do you need me to put a good word in for you at the places I'ma try to get into?"

Madison shook her head. "I'm done. I'm throwing my G-string away. Getting fired was the best thing that could have happened. It pushed me out since I couldn't build up the nerve to walk out."

Nancy smiled. Finally, Madison's life was taking a turn for the better. She understood nothing about what was going on. Madison gave her limited details, but if it meant Madison leaving stripping alone for good and no longer tripping back into a world she didn't belong in from the beginning, then this move was the right choice and long overdue.

"Where does she live?" Nancy asked.

Madison never looked at Nancy. It was questions such as those she wished to avoid. This new world she was entering wasn't open. It wasn't verbal nor social. It was closed off and unpredictable, and if Madison wanted in, she would have to adapt to not knowing everything.

"My sister is very private, so don't be surprised if I'm the one visiting you."

Nancy sat quietly. Change was never easy for her, but obviously, this was one thing she'd have to ride with.

"Okay then." Nancy stood up, her fingers snapping. This new chapter of her friend's life was not meant for her to read, so she allowed it to be Madison's diary. "Let me help you pack. Where should I begin?" She looked around at the disarray, anxious to jump in and get this show on the road.

"You can start with the bookshelf." Madison nodded toward the five large bookshelves overflowing with books.

Nancy looked at the selection of genres and scrunched up her face. "I'ma be boxing those books all night."

Madison shrugged her shoulders and smiled. "You wanted to help."

While in the process of building a box, Nancy's attitude changed. She had just remembered that she was jobless because of ex-coworkers.

"I want to get them back." Nancy's head moved from side to side as she plucked books off the shelf and allowed them to fall to the floor. One by one, each hardback slammed onto the floor and canceled out the quietness in Madison's home.

Closing her eyes due to the loud disturbance, Madison found herself thinking back to when all she wanted was revenge and how she missed out on her chance, realizing it wasn't worth it.

"It's not worth it!" Madison yelled. Her voice rose in order to talk over the loud thuds erupting from the falling books.

"What?" Nancy stopped dropping the books and looked at the side of Madison's face. A sea of objects was scattered on the floor, separating the two.

"It's not worth it," Madison repeated.

Nancy smirked. She threw five more books on the floor just to annoy Madison because of her comment and then flopped herself down on the floor where she would fill her first box up with reading material. For two minutes, no one said anything. However, each time Nancy shook her head over her disgrace with Madison, the closer she came to voicing her thoughts.

"They put us through hell and then had the nerve to get us fired. How can it not be worth it?" Nancy finally let out.

Without turning fully in Nancy's direction, Madison looked at her through the corner of her eye and replied simply by saying, "Because it's not."

Nancy laughed. Madison's new way of thinking was baffling. However, she knew she'd come to understand it in due time. Taping up the box and pushing the conversation she and her friend had agreed to disagree on to the side, Madison changed the subject.

"If I put in for gas, would you take me to Long Island tomorrow?"

"You going to your aunt's?"

"Nah, my sister's."

"I thought she didn't want anyone coming by her house," Nancy reminded Madison.

"She doesn't want anyone coming by the house we're moving into. I'm sure she doesn't care about *this* house. We'll be gone soon."

"Fine," Nancy agreed.

Madison leaned back against the couch, exhaustion filling her body. "I'm tired. Want to take a break?"

Chapter 32

Although Renee used them, crooked cops nauseated her. It was sad what this world had come to. The actions of cops were no longer what they signed up to oblige and wound up doing more harm than good. Renee rewound back to the behavior she exhibited these past few years and felt a knot grow in the center of her chest. All these years had passed, and still nothing had changed. She had forced an infected man to contaminate others and killed all in one day. This was not a way of life, not a way to grow old and plan a future around. Renee took a deep breath, her concentration dedicated to the road, while her heart sat in the center of hysteria.

What would pull her out of this world and keep her away? She double blinked, pushing tears back inside of their ducts. The thought of a child calmed and soothed her. Turning down the corner leading to her home, Renee entertained the thought of having a child. The thought caused her to smile. She looked at her home from a distance. The calmness it reflected was another reason she missed Manhattan. This place was too quiet, too slow, too unpredictable. Pulling into the driveway, she noticed her front door was wide open, and now she wondered how calm of a place her neighborhood really was.

A dark house was one thing Renee and Julian didn't do. Whether the house was fully or partially lit, they needed light. So while Renee peered inside the dark house from the door, she knew something was wrong. Walking inside, she pulled her gun out of her coat pocket and lightly pushed the door shut. There was only one person who would come for her, and Renee wanted her badly. Locked inside, the two would battle over who would not only walk away with the crown, but their life.

Renee used the darkness to her advantage. Walking toward the staircase, she tripped and lost her balance, her arms wrapping around the railing she used for stability. Stretching out her leg, she gently tapped her shoe against the floor, stepping on what felt like something big and hard. She used the tip of her shoe to push it. When no movement occurred, she dug inside her pants pocket and used her cell phone for light. Lighting the area with a ray of white, she saw her shoes covered in blood and a body whose face was unrecognizable. The clothing covering the corpse was what caused Renee to escape reality and her body to break out in chills.

Frantic, she let go of the railing, and the puddle of blood lubricating the bottom of her shoes caused her to slip and land on the steps completely, her butt meeting the stairs. Now at the level of the body, she grabbed his head and searched for a clue as to who he was. The clothing Julian wore earlier that day was not enough to bring her fears to life. She stared into the bashed-in face and saw nothing that would help her determine who he was. He had been beaten to the point where facial features were now demolished, and it was then her refusal to believe this was him had faded. His body type, complexion, and anything else people would search for in order to identify a loved one all led back to Julian.

The room started to spin, and hot tears heated Renee's face. Flesh and bones slid from where his cheek used to be and dropped onto Renee's hand. There she sat mentally far away in a trance where she raced through a meadow. It was so bright, so clear and multicolored, her feet took off like a runner's, and the wind she created rustled the grass and wildflowers. She couldn't stop running and allowed her mind to run into the unknown. A forest of trees came into view, and before Renee entered the giant's realm, she snapped back to two years ago.

"Why would someone get a tattoo of a bunch of trees?" Julian's voice seeped inside of her eardrums, a past conversation about a stranger's tattoo exploding in her ears. In a haste, she lifted Julian's sleeve until his right shoulder was revealed. The sight of it caused her to cry harder and her head to drop onto what was left of the corpse's forehead. Renee's space in time to where she was preparing to lose her mind made her remember to search for a tattoo. There was not one on the man's arm. It was not Julian.

"She's crying." Carmen looked up at the ceiling from down in the basement. She beamed off the sound of Renee's pain. "She thinks he's you."

After a moment of living in her accomplishment of outsmarting Renee, Carmen finally looked at an unconscious Julian tied to a chair. She spoke to a man who heard nothing. Julian's new attire was courtesy of Roy, and the huge knot sticking out of his head saddened Carmen just by the sight. She walked over to him and gently stroked it.

"I'm sorry I hit you, but you would have killed him."

Her hand froze in place, and when she thought about it, she figured it wouldn't have mattered if Julian killed Roy, since she killed him minutes after knocking Julian out anyway. If there was one thing Carmen didn't forget, it was Julian. The entire time she ran around New York and Miami rampant, she always thought of him and always kept it in the back of her mind to continue with their relationship once bigger matters such as Renee were handled.

However, by the appearance of it all, their time together would never come. She had underestimated Renee. Her need for greed dumped her into an environment she could not adapt to, and now that she had acknowledged and accepted this, she decided to force Julian into her hands.

The smart way of getting back at Renee and causing her very being to collapse would have been for Carmen to harm Julian when she had the chance, but she couldn't. Instead, she got him off her uncle, and in the process of helping Roy up, she looked down at Julian. Lying there, everything she had ever felt for him grew, and everything of Renee's she had ever wanted screamed in her ears.

Looking at her uncle struggling to get himself together, Carmen picked up the shovel she dropped after attacking Julian and began to slam it into his face. Over and over again, she hit Roy until his facial features were unrecognizable. After both men were on the floor unconscious, Carmen stripped the two of their clothes and switched their outfits. She then took the handle of the shovel and stabbed Roy in the chest, ensuring that he was dead. Leaving Roy where he lay, Carmen dragged Julian down into the basement as carefully as she could, happy to finally have him.

Stroking Julian's head, Carmen told him, "I'm glad I got you off him, because if I didn't, I would have never discovered just how strong my feelings for you are. And after seeing what he'd done to you, I had to hurt him just as much as he hurt you."

Carmen gazed into Julian's face and briefly experienced a slideshow of Benz's and Lincoln's faces flashing on and off in front of her. Shocked by the images, her eyes widened and her lips parted, lost in the sight of her past. Julian's head movements went unnoticed.

Coming to, the first thing he saw was the bloody shovel propped up against the wall, blood flowing down the handle and landing on the floor. He turned his head and saw Carmen staring at him. She wasn't blinking or talking. In fact, it looked like she wasn't in this world. Infuriated by her presence, Julian tried jumping from his seat so that he could punish her for everything she had put him through, but when his chest pumped up and his legs and arms didn't move, he toppled over in his seat.

The sound of him crashing against the floor pulled Carmen out of her trance slideshow.

Wiggling on the floor while trying to free himself, Julian yelled, "Un-fuckin'-tie me!" His screams emulated a lion's roar.

The intensity and aggression in his voice sent shock waves inside of Carmen. Julian continued screaming, his need to be free breaking through in his voice. Carmen stood back, her better judgment telling her not to untie a thing.

Julian saw the skeptical, nervous look on her face. He yelled some more, angry that she was now showing fear over what she created. "Untie me!"

Stuck where she stood, Carmen said nothing. It had been a long time since she'd heard him speak to her, so she replayed his demands in her head, savoring his voice. Loving the sound, she smiled. "No. I have to come out of this with something, and I chose you." Carmen had lost everything, but if she gained Julian, she'd gain it all.

"You don't want me, because the moment you untie me, I am going to choke the life out of you. I am going to squeeze your neck slowly, and every time you're seconds from blacking out, I am going to release my hold only to tighten my grip and do it all over again once you regain consciousness. I am going to repeat that over and over until I get bored and then never let go."

Carmen stomped over toward Julian, unlike any other time she was in control. Carmen pulled the sweater she wore off her back and dropped it on the panels. "One more time," she whispered in his ear. The distance they once had, Julian missed. "One more time."

Plopping herself on his lap, Carmen grabbed his chin and forced their lips to meet. Julian tore away from her grasp, a sickening and irate glare filling his eyes. Carmen undid his fly and released the organ responsible for her addiction to him.

"One more time," Carmen repeated.

While stroking his member with one hand, Carmen used the other to untie the string of her sweatpants. After pulling them below her waist, she used the tips of her toes to give her the boost she needed to mount what belonged to Renee. Before entering Carmen, Julian felt the hair on her vagina tickle his penis. The intimate jester from another woman stirred up vomit within his stomach, but the blood racing to his penis pushed all common sense out of his brain.

"Come here," he demanded.

Carmen's upper body remained in the air, her legs slightly shaking due to holding up her weight. "What?"

"Come here and kiss me again," Julian instructed, his breathing heavy and his eyes fluttering.

Closed eyes and a stiff rod gave away that Julian had thrown up the white flag. This was the Julian she remembered from the plane. The Julian who confirmed she was doing her job as a seductress. The sight of her body and the attention given to his staff sent Julian to a place that would give him satisfaction.

Closing her eyes, Carmen leaned into Julian. Once her top and bottom eyelashes touched and her eyes closed, Julian's opened, and he bit into her face the second Carmen was close enough. Carmen yelled, the feeling of teeth breaking into flesh overwhelming her and forcing her to try to pull away. But whenever she tried to back away, Julian leaned forward, following her. The hold he had on her face was sturdy and secure. The sight of Carmen's body and the feel of her skin planted the idea of ripping off her face. He had to rip her apart like she tried doing to his and Renee's relationship.

Julian crunched down harder into her nose and cheek, blood escaped, and the added pain caused Carmen to punch at his body. "Let me go! Let me go!" Carmen's screams rocked the house's foundation, the need to be released intensifying with every second. "Get off me! Get off me!"

The laughs seeping from the corners of Julian's mouth were what loosened his hold. After several tugs, Carmen's flesh slipped away, and Carmen stumbled backward. She grabbed her face, and blood quickly covered her hands, giving the illusion that she was wearing red gloves. Screaming, while in tears, Carmen struggled to plug the large piece of flesh hanging from her face back into where it belonged.

With a mouth full of blood and a pinch of happiness, Julian laughed. He laughed long and hard over Carmen's pain, blood leaking out of the corners of his mouth and his fingers tugging at the ropes that were coming loose.

Chapter 33

Shaking and afraid of what she may see, Carmen finally opened her eyes and looked at her hands. They were soaked in blood along with small chunks of skin, which were removed from her face. Without looking at Julian, she nodded her head the entire walk toward the shovel. Picking it up once again, it had become her dependent, her best friend, and the only one in the world who seemed to do her right.

She dragged it Julian's way, and he continued to laugh. It was the distant look in her eyes and the quietness she gave that led him to believe that she had finally crossed over into a world no one thought she'd fit into, but it was too late. Her proving her might added no points to her roster and left her at zero. So Julian continued to laugh and wouldn't stop until he was content. He laughed until Carmen stood in front of him. He laughed until Carmen lifted the shovel as high as she could. He laughed until she swung it, the wind it created whistling in the air. He laughed until he watched Carmen drop to the floor, the bullets that entered her drawing new blood that blemished even wood.

After shooting, Renee chucked the firearm across the room. She had dropped the beast, and now it was time to lay the dog down. Fluttering on the floor with her left hand covering her wounded shoulder the bullet went through, Carmen whimpered. She tried her best not to exhibit how much pain she was really in. Renee had won so much, so why give her more?

"You missed," Carmen chuckled, her lips forming into a smile.

Taking the position of a catcher, Renee kneeled down beside Carmen. "I didn't miss," Renee growled. "I want your ass alive."

Killing Carmen could have been quick, but what would have been the excitement in that? She wanted Carmen to suffer. Renee needed to release years of depression from her soul. Throwing Carmen's hand off her injury, Renee stabbed her finger inside of the bullet hole. Carmen's body became erect, and the screams escaping her mouth sent shockwaves throughout the room. Her body froze, and although she wanted to push Renee away, she couldn't. The pain was paralyzing and heart-wrenching. Renee pushed her finger as deep as physically possible inside of the wound and wiggled it. She then grabbed Carmen's head and held it in place.

"You wanna be the queen? Then man up!" she spat.

Removing her finger from the wound, she dropped to her knees and wrapped both hands around Carmen's neck. The thought of watching and feeling life flee from her body was what kept Renee sane. The thought of the cat finally catching the mouse sent her to a new world. She had to take away something as special as life from the person who took so much from her. Renee's eyes bulged out, her neck outstretched, and her arms and face began to tremble. She would end the poison flowing through her life, and she would love it.

"You're a leech. Everything you touch falls apart. I'ma take pleasure in watching you crumble!" Renee expressed.

Renee squeezed her neck tighter. She finally had her, and there was no way she was going to let her go. Carmen kicked violently. Her nails dug into Renee's hands and drew little globules of blood. Weak from being shot, Carmen became exasperated. With everything she had in her, she directed her energy into the kick she was prepared to let out.

Repositioning her body as much as she could, Carmen aligned her leg with Renee and kicked, the strength exploding from deep within. The force in Renee's stomach pushed her away. Her hands unlocked from around Carmen's neck in an effort to break her fall. Watching Renee dive backward, Carmen pushed herself up with her one good arm and stood to her feet. Standing over Renee, she gave the last laugh and shoved her foot into her neck, pinning Renee's head against the floor. Carmen smiled.

"You're not so strong, not so scary."

Renee's hands grabbed the sides of Carmen's ankle and tried to lift her foot from her neck. The more she pushed, the more weight Carmen placed on her neck.

"Go to sleep, go to sleep. Oh, I'm sorry, you probably don't know that song. It was designated only for me whenever our father came around."

Carmen pushed her foot deeper into Renee's neck, the blockage of air forcing her eyes to close and her hands to unwrap from around Carmen's ankle.

"Go the fuck to sleep!" Carmen snarled.

She put her entire weight onto that one leg, her free leg now dangling in the air. Renee couldn't breathe, and she couldn't fight. All she could do was allow her hands to hit the floorboard. Seconds before the end, Carmen was pulled from her feet, the room spinning as her body was swung in the air and her face smashed into the wall like a human ragdoll. Her body slithered down to the floor, the lullaby she sang turning against her and now putting her to sleep.

Julian stood over Carmen, his breathing off beat and his eyes twitching. The ropes that once confined him were no more than a puddle beneath the chair he was once tied to.

***

The smell of the Jeep never changed. The stale scent of death infested the seat cushions, and the scratches plunged inside of the car doors tattooed the interior. The Jeep was always quiet, and when you sat in its seats, you agreed to its code of silence. You'd drive through the streets and look out of its windows at people who couldn't make out your face from behind the tint. It was a moment stuck in time you'd never get back. A moment you'd hold on to but lock away in your subconscious.

Renee looked out the window, rocks from beneath the tires exploding in every direction. She saw nothing. It was the darkest hour of the night, and they drove through dirt as smoothly as the dirt path allowed. Renee looked to her left and temporarily watched Dane, who was in her own little world while playing chauffeur. Julian sat behind Dane's seat, his posture never changing during the thirty-minute drive. Renee laid her head back, her discolored skin a goodbye gift from Carmen. She closed her eyes. This was peace. This was the end of a life she had chosen but didn't truly want. Happiness did not come from misery. It came from deep within, and if Renee were ever to achieve it, she had to allow the positivity in. She had to live life on God's terms.

And then the banging started. Carmen would not let go of the rhythm she had adopted since being thrown into the trunk. Renee's eyes opened, and annoyance filled her irises. Dane sped up. Her increase in speed warned Renee and Julian to hang on. Abruptly, the car stopped short, and a large bang surged from the trunk of the car.

Carmen's impaired shoulder took another hit against the car's interior for a third time. Her eyes shut, and her lips trembled. The tears against her cheeks were dry and white. Carmen's body felt like a piñata. She was beaten, bruised, and worn on the outside. Every time she was hit, her banging for help seemed equivalent to moving a mountain.

Once silence was yet again obtained, Renee closed her eyes and enjoyed the ride. This was why Carmen was in the position she was in. She didn't know the rules, didn't care to learn them, and damn sure didn't respect whatever knowledge she gained. It was an unwritten rule for silence to occur whenever Dane was behind the wheel of the big black Jeep. This was a job that was long overdue. So while driving to their destination, the three wanted nothing more than to savor the moment and look forward to what was about to occur.

When the car came to a halt, the cold night's air knocked softly on the windows. Each door opened, and without looking behind them, Renee and Julian walked forward with a total of three shovels. The crackling sounds of twigs and hard stones created music sinking underneath their feet. Standing beside the burial plot, the two waited for a kicking and uncontrollable Carmen to appear. Carmen's eyes enlarged when Dane forced her tied upper body to walk up to the six-foot hole.

"Let me go. Let me the fuck go!" she wailed. Carmen's body twisted and turned. She fought against the discomfort splashing through her body and the cold weather nipping at her open wounds. "I'll leave. I'll go somewhere far away so you'll never see me again. I promise!" she pleaded. Tears raced down her cheeks. Salt burned where her skin once covered. "Please! Please! Renee, I'm your sister!"

There was no casket in the ditch, only dirt. Carmen knew what was to come, and her heart couldn't slow its pace. Looking around, her eyes adjusted to the dark and allowed her to see countless headstones throughout the cemetery. She shook, and her legs weakened beneath her.

"Sisters don't do what you do," Renee expressed. The frosty tone of her voice withered away, and for once, she gave her heart permission to speak. She looked Carmen in the eye. When Carmen met her stare, the corners of their mouths dropped, and their eyes twinkled with tears ready to escape. However, each was held hostage by the woman whose body they belonged to.

"I wanted a sister, and I'm sorry she couldn't have been you," Renee honestly admitted.

Although Renee wasn't excited when she first met Carmen, it was a soothing feeling to have a relative around. Renee always wanted family, so when she looked at Carmen, there were times she saw Page and hoped to form a sisterhood, something she didn't have with Page. It would have taken a lot to have gotten to that point, but secretly Renee was ready to put in the effort. However, none of that happened. Carmen didn't want to live in harmony. She wanted to live in selfishness, and that one quality was what destroyed a beautiful sibling bond that could have been.

Carmen broke down, and her heart shattered. Could things have been different if her intentions had been pure? Could she have had it all and then some? Did she kick herself out of having a happy, family-united life? Could there have actually been hope for her? And if so, had she turned it away during her race to achieve the material things in life? For as long as Carmen could remember, she always wanted her father. She always wanted her family to be complete and for her father and Madison to live with her. Now looking at Renee, her older sister, who was fighting back her emotions, she realized she had chosen anger over love. Looking into her eyes, Carmen asked lastly, "Can you give me another chance?"

It was an honest question, a hard question, but nonetheless, a question that needed to be asked because it was asked from the heart.

"No," Renee whispered.

Her answer was low and barely audible, yet everyone heard. Carmen nodded her head, not because she agreed with Renee's decision, but because she knew, had the shoe been on the other foot, she too would have answered no. Standing tall, Carmen flushed out all her emotions and repented her sins out loud. She now understood the definition of true happiness, and although these were her last seconds on this earth, she'd live them right. After asking God for forgiveness, she looked back at Renee, then at Julian and Dane.

"I'm sorry," she told them.

By the heavy rope holding Carmen's wrists behind her back, Dane shoved her into the hole. Crashing into the dirt, Carmen felt her arm snap. She opened her mouth and howled, dirt racing into her mouth from the wall of dirt her face was pressed up against.

In the fetal position, Carmen alternated between crying and screaming in agony. With the same shovel Carmen killed with, Dane used to cover her in dirt. It took a long time for the hole to be filled, but eventually, it was. Sweating and covered in dirt, Julian and Dane dragged their shovels back with them to the car. Walking slowly behind them, Renee stopped and listened closely. It was low, very low, but Renee could still hear her sister yelling for help.

Chapter 34

Two Years Later

Calm. That was a word Renee hadn't used or experienced in a long time. The clear Tahiti water rocked back and forth. From behind her sunglasses, she finally saw the view of the ocean that was normally achieved only when receiving a postcard that read, "Wish you were here." Renee dug her feet into the hot sand and welcomed the therapeutic feeling it gave her toes. Julian's thick hand held hers, his thumb rubbing her hand. Renee took in the love, releasing what had been and appreciating what was.

"What are you thinking about?" Julian asked tenderly.

"Nothing. For once, nothing." She closed her eyes, reopened them, and felt a wave of positivity. She thanked God for this moment, for her strength, and more importantly, achieving happiness. "Once upon a time, it would have been something related to business, but now it's nothing, absolutely nothing." Peace of mind was a rare ingredient of life. It was delicate, desired, and often mistreated, but when handled with care, it was a blessing.

"Are you nervous about returning to the States?" Julian asked, her reflection filling his sunglasses.

"A little, but I think Nancy has everything under control." Renee smiled. "She filled my shoes quite nicely." The thought of a white girl being her protégé stretched her smile out farther. The vision Renee had pertaining to who would fill her shoes had become fully reconstructed after time spent with Nancy. Nancy's personality traits revealed to Renee that she needed someone out of the box, a fresh, unpredictable dictator for the drug world.

Nancy was a rare breed, capable of changing a game that hadn't been shaken in quite some time. She was hungry, held a colorful personality that kept her off the radar, and was heavily underestimated, let alone never perceived as a contestant in the drug business because of her gender and race. Everything about Nancy that made the underworld turn up their noises was what made Renee select her. That and she was business savvy. Renee preferred to walk away with nothing except the shirt on her back, leaving the past in the past. However, as a show of appreciation and ongoing loyalty, Nancy demanded that Renee receive a percentage of her earnings paired with monthly updates. She had taken the word "protégé" to new heights.

"I agree. For once, I'm happy with your decision on who will take over." Julian smiled, comfortable in the fact that this time he had a say in what transpired due to Renee's exit. A brief flashback on his reaction to Renee crowning Carmen her protégé came to mind.

Renee laughed. "Don't remind me. I was hesitant at first. Nancy was a stranger, but then again, so was Carmen, so I saw no reason not to give someone I wasn't related to a shot. Nancy's proven to be a good addition to the team in ways we hadn't even expected."

Julian nodded his head, his finger gliding over the two-carat diamond square ring on Renee's ring finger.

"Na, this ring is a good addition to the team, and this honeymoon is the icing on the cake."

Renee took her sunglasses off and smiled at him. Finally, she was happy.

Discussion Questions

1. Did you agree with Dane and Metro's reasoning for dethroning Renee?

2. If only one of the twins could have survived, who would you have liked to see live and why?

3. When meeting Madison, did you believe she was sincere or another snake in the grass?

4. If you could have kept one character in this novel from dying, who would it have been and why?

5. Do you believe Raquel was justified in telling Dane where Carmen lived?

6. Did Jared's death surprise you? Why or why not?

7. What ran through your mind while reading the HIV club scene?

8. Would Renee have been better off had she left the game alone when Dane and Metro dethroned her?

9. Do you think Madison was too hard on Carmen?

10. How did you predict this book ending?

About the Author

Born and raised in New York City, where she lives with her husband, Brandie Davis-White graduated with a bachelor's degree in English from York College and is the founder of My Urban Books blog and Facebook book club. From home, she continues to pen drama-filled novels.

Follow Brandie on Facebook at:
www.facebook.com/brandie.davis.948

Join her Facebook book club My Urban Books Club at:
www.facebook.com/groups/232356380133003/

Twitter: @AuthorBrandieD

Instagram: @authorbrandiedavis